I0719737

A Nose for a Niedeman

Anne Louise Bannon

Healcroft House, Publishers

Healcroft House, Publishers,
a subsidiary of Robin Goodfellow Enterprises
2591 N. Fair Oaks Ave., #408
Altadena, CA, 91001
626-502-7416
United States of America

Library of Congress Control Number:
2018911951

ISBN: 978-1-948616-03-4

Dedication

To the Sisters in Crime – thanks for everything!

The picture dominated the room. It was not a part of the room. It was stark and modern, and completely out of place, which is why it was the first thing I saw.

The room had a comfortable feel to it, in spite of its precision neatness. The gray and rust pillows on the dark blue overstuffed sofa were perfectly aligned with the corners. A Waterford crystal lamp stood on the exact center of the dark oak top on each of two end tables. Two printed velvet wingback chairs rested at a forty-five-degree angle with another dark oak table between them. A quilted reproduction of Van Gogh's "The Harvest" watched from the wall above the sofa. Ninety degrees away, on the adjacent wall, an intricately carved marble mantelpiece framed a brick fireplace.

The picture sat on a brass easel in front of the fireplace. Aesthetics aside, it seemed a rather awkward place for it. Not that I was in any position to question it, or rather, I didn't think I was in any position to. I had yet to meet Mrs. Sperling.

She'd hired me the day before as her chauffeur, over the phone. Her attorney had handled all the paperwork: my DMV sheet, insurance, driver's license. It seemed pretty strange. After all, it was a live-in position. I'd asked her if she wanted to meet me first, and she laughed and said it would be pointless, but maybe I'd like to meet her. So, there I was, in her living room, wondering why she had that huge picture on the easel.

I'd been shown through the entry hall into the room by a young man in his early twenties, if that old. He was tall but didn't look it, with light brown hair and dressed in a trendy baggy gray sweater and faded black jeans.

He returned, and carefully adjusted the huge lace doily on the back of the sofa.

"Mrs. S. will be down in a minute," he said in his soft tenor voice.

"Fine," I replied. I had arrived a couple minutes early.

On his way to the wingback chairs, he passed the picture, glanced at it, and sighed.

"I know," I said. "It really doesn't belong in here."

He looked around. "Oo. It doesn't." He shook his head and shrugged. "That's not why it's here anyway."

He sighed again and moved a pink Wedgwood vase a microscopic bit towards the center of the table between the two wingbacks. He noticed my puzzled look.

"A sixteenth of an inch can mean the difference between an intact vase and me paying for one," he explained. "Mrs. S. totally has to be that tough.

It's like she'd never get through the house if everything wasn't exactly where she knew it was gonna be."

"Oh." I still didn't understand, but I decided Mrs. Sperling would enlighten me.

"By the way, my name's Glen." He smiled.

"I'm Donna."

"I know. You told me when you came in."

"Oh. That's right."

I heard a quick clicking sound from the hallway and turned towards it. A yellow Labrador retriever trotted into the room. Mrs. Sperling had asked me if I liked dogs, which I do.

"Eleanor," Glen addressed the dog. "You're supposed to be upstairs."

The Lab cocked her head at me.

"It's alright, Glen," called Mrs. Sperling's voice, pleasant and well-bred, even at a higher volume.

Eleanor approached me. I held out my hand for her to sniff. She seemed to approve. I scratched her throat.

"She wanted to meet Donna," Mrs. Sperling continued as she entered the room.

She was of average height. Her elegantly tailored pale blue suit covered a somewhat padded figure. She had dark blonde hair with wisps of gray running through it, cut into what they used to call a wedge. There was something very graceful about the way she moved, which covered up how fast she did it.

She smiled knowingly at Glen. "Are you also interested in joining us?"

"For sure," Glen replied. His attitude towards his boss was respectful but relaxed and friendly. "I mean, a new roommate and all."

"Very well. By the way, the hall lamp…"

"Oh!" he groaned. "I'm really trying!"

"There was no damage done this time, fortunately. And don't worry about it. You're much further along than your predecessor was when she left, and she'd worked here five years." She turned and addressed the air next to Glen. "So, you're Donna Brechter."

"Yes."

She shifted to face me. There was something not quite right about her eyes.

"I'm Delilah Sperling," she said and stepped forward to shake my hand.

I closed in and took hers. "It's nice to meet you, Mrs. Sperling."

"The pleasure is mutual. Should I have Glen show you around, or do you have any questions?"

"Not really." I looked around a little nervously.

Mrs. Sperling chuckled. "You're wondering who I am and if I'm on the right side of the law."

"No!" I blushed. "Well, a little. It just seemed weird that you were satisfied with a phone interview, that you didn't want to see me first."

"I said it would be pointless." Mrs. Sperling seemed to be enjoying some joke that I had missed. Even Glen was in on it. "But if you think it's that important, why don't you describe yourself."

"How?"

"Physically, your appearance."

That stumped me. After all, I was standing right in front of her. Then it dawned on me. Her eyes weren't quite right. The left one was clouded over and unfocused. The right eye looked inward and twitched steadily.

"Sure." I took a deep breath. "I'm five-eight, one hundred and twenty pounds. I've got brown hair, blue eyes. My hair's real long, down to my waist. I've got very long arms and legs. Frankly, if I could only use one word to describe myself, that would be it: long."

Mrs. Sperling chuckled. "Indeed. I believe you said you are a dancer?"

"Only when it doesn't interfere with my work here," I said quickly.

"I doubt it will. But why chauffeuring?"

"I heard the money was good, and I like to drive. I don't mind odd hours, either."

"Excellent." She smiled. "Not that I expect there'll be many of them. I lead a quieter life than most of my peers."

Glen snickered.

"I do lead a quieter life," Mrs. Sperling insisted.

"You just don't party," said Glen.

Mrs. Sperling sighed and turned back to me. "The picture on the easel. Would you try to describe it for me?"

I looked at it carefully. "Well, it's a print, a real good one. Um. It's a picture of a woman with her hair pinned up and wearing a beaded necklace and nothing else. The picture stops at her waist. Um. Do you mind if I ask how much you can see, and how long you've been that way?"

Her eyebrow lifted. "I am completely blind and have been since birth. Why do you ask?"

I swallowed. "I just wanted to know if color meant anything to you."

"A valid question. Color does have meaning, but I suspect not in quite the same way it would for you. For me, blue is water or cold ice. Red is blood, warm and sticky."

"Yeah. I think I got it. Um. The woman's skin is white, like a crisp sheet. She's very sharply defined with black lines... Um, like a narrow rail. The style is almost realistic, maybe like the difference between an ancient Greek sculpture and something from the twentieth century. The necklace is burgundy, like wine, and so are her lips. Her eyes are blue like velvet or flowers. The background is grayish blue, almost a gunmetal color. Surrounding the whole thing is a border that's gray like satin. The bottom border is much wider than the rest, and it has Niedeman written on it in black."

"That's sufficient." Mrs. Sperling seemed to be laughing. "You did very well, Donna. Do you think you can continue along those lines for me?"

"Sure."

"This shall work out better than I thought. That picture is a limited-edition serigraph by the late artist, Hans Niedeman. He was the American-born son of German immigrants and only died roughly two years ago. Since that time, his widow released a series of fifteen limited edition commemorative serigraphs of his work. This is HN4. Glen obtained it the other day through a special arrangement."

"He got a good deal?" I asked.

"Not really. It's a fake."

"Oh." I grimaced as Glen sighed.

"It's an excellent forgery," continued Mrs. Sperling. "I'm told the counterfeiter even got the texture right. But genuine Niedeman serigraphs have a distinctive smell that this one does not." She paused for a moment. "Do you have any further questions?"

"No."

"Would you care to see your rooms?"

"Unless you've got someplace you want to go first."

"Yes, I think I would prefer to." She nodded. "Thank you. After you sign your W-2s and insurance papers, please help Glen wrap the Niedeman. We are going to confront Mr. Joshua Stein."

"The gentleman who sold Glen the Niedeman?" I cocked a hopeful grin at her.

Her eyebrow lifted and she smiled. "Yes."

The paperwork didn't take long to fill out. I was happy to be employed, and it looked like the job would be a lot of fun, not to mention the major advantage of moving out of my folks' place. My parents wanted me out. Well, I was twenty-six, the oldest, and the only one of my siblings still living at home.

Glen appeared with a long sheet of brown wrapping paper. It was a bit of a struggle getting the paper around the frame. The picture was more awkward than heavy. Mrs. Sperling entered the room as we finished, Eleanor at her side in the traditional harness.

"Shall we be going?" she asked. She handed me a full keychain. "Here are your keys, Donna. We'll go ahead and take the Lexus. We don't want to be too intimidating. That key is on the opposite end of the ring from the housekeys."

"Thank you."

The keychain was a large split ring on a leather strap, with the three housekeys on one side and the fobs for the cars on the right. The car was a silver four-door Lexus LS hybrid. The darned thing even talked to me, reminding me to put on my seat belt. I didn't even have any trouble hooking it up to my phone.

Mrs. Sperling sat up front with me, and Glen sat in the back with Eleanor. There's always plenty of traffic in L.A., even in Beverly Hills. However, that morning it was lighter than normal. We made good time.

It was a gorgeous November day, with brilliant blue skies, and crisp nippy air. It had been cold the past few nights. The days didn't warm up that much, either. We'd had rain the week before, and the nearby mountains were sporting white tops.

The studio we wanted was in the Rodeo Drive district, a couple blocks over from Rodeo, itself. The building was at the end of the block. It was a tan brick edifice with three stories that had been built sometime in the 1940s, I guessed. There was a door built into the corner leading into a narrow foyer with a spiral staircase in front of an elevator, and another glass-fronted door leading into the gallery. That door was locked.

"That's odd," mused Mrs. Sperling.

I shivered. It was surprisingly cold in the foyer.

"It should be open," Glen said. "It was yesterday."

I pressed against the glass with shaded eyes. "It's not today. There's no one in there, and no lights on. Wait. I think there's a light coming from the back."

"Then that's where we'll go." Mrs. Sperling turned and swung her arm in front of her. "Eleanor, forward."

We went around the corner to the alley that ran behind the block. The building's back door was easy to find. It was open, but not to the studio. That door was next to a flight of stairs that led into the rest of the building.

"Hello?" Mrs. Sperling called. She lightly felt along the wall and tried the studio door. It was locked tight. She banged on it. "Hello?"

"Hey! Who the hell's down there?" The voice came from outside and above.

Mrs. Sperling, Eleanor, Glen, and I stumbled over each other going outside.

"Excuse us, sir," Mrs. Sperling addressed the roof. "We're looking for Mr. Stein."

A round head of dark curly hair appeared over the edge.

"You are? Why? The building's closed."

"It is?" Mrs. Sperling asked. "We were just out front, and it appears there's a light on in the back. Could it be that Mr. Stein is here after all?"

"A light, huh." The head disappeared. A few seconds later we heard bumping feet on the stairs, and the head with the rest of its body arrived. He was short and paunchy and wearing a Twisted Sister t-shirt with faded 501 jeans.

"We'd be open, but there was a big problem yesterday afternoon," he said going through a set of keys. "Uh, power failure." He looked up at us. "I'm Kyle Hoffman, the building manager."

He chose a key and opened the door. Mrs. Sperling went in first. She sniffed and frowned. Eleanor growled softly, then whined. I stepped in and looked around.

"He's not here," I said, shivering again. It wasn't any warmer in the gallery back room.

"I think he may be." Mrs. Sperling had a strange, grim half-smile on her face as if the situation both excited and repulsed her.

Glen pushed his way in. "Look!" He pointed. "An HN4!" He scrambled over to the middle of the room, where there was a table with a long, flat wooden box on it. Above it was hanging the Niedeman serigraph. "We've got him... Oh, my God!"

Glen came reeling back, his face a pale green color. I foolishly went to see what had gotten him that way. I came back the same color.

"I assume you've discovered why the studio is

not open," Mrs. Sperling said.

"Oh, you betcha," I groaned. "He's awful red, but I think he's dead."

The first thing Mrs. Sperling did was send Kyle Hoffman to phone the police. The second thing was to have me describe the room and all its contents. She and Glen stood in the doorway, while I looked the space over from just in front of them.

"Well, it's very plain," I said, nervously. "Do you want size?"

"Judging from the echoes, I'd say approximately four hundred square feet." Mrs. Sperling answered. "Glen?"

"Uh, yeah, close to that." Glen was trying not to panic.

"Okay." I swallowed. "On the wall opposite to us is an old camp cot with a six-inch-thick mattress, all made up perfectly with a dark green army blanket. The wall next to the street has three windows, all open, and there's a birdcage and parakeet next to the center one. There's bird seed all over the place. There's a door in the wall facing the windows, and all sorts of shelves with pictures in them. Behind you is a desk with tons of papers on it, and more bird seed, et cetera."

"Interesting," murmured Mrs. Sperling.

"In the center of the room," I continued. "Are

two long tables like you find in school multi-purpose rooms. On the furthest one is a flat wooden box with screens…"

"A silk-screening apparatus," Glen cut in.

"So, I surmised," answered Mrs. Sperling. "Are the inks there also?"

"Six or seven jars of them," I said. "And the previously mentioned serigraph hanging to the right of the box. The, uh, body is lying between the two tables. The nearer one has several frame pieces, more papers and a hot plate on it, and what looks like left-over bread on a paper plate."

"Describe the body."

"The body?" I balked. "It's a man, and he's real red."

"Carbon monoxide poisoning." Mrs. Sperling nodded. "What is he wearing?"

"Clothes."

"Would you look again at the body and give me a more accurate description? Just make sure you take the same path that you did to find him.

Gulping back all sorts of obscenities, I did as I was asked.

"Alright. He's wearing dark brown high-waisted pants, brown like rich soil, blue, tan and yellow paisley big shirt, paisley is like a bent over teardrop shape, brown suspenders, a brown tweed sloppy cardigan, black socks and brown loafers."

"There's something wrong there." Mrs. Sperling frowned. "But I can't think what."

She frowned, then sniffed discreetly.

Sirens approached as Hoffman wandered up behind Mrs. Sperling and Glen.

"Cops are on their way," he announced needlessly. He glanced at Mrs. Sperling, then whispered to Glen, "What's she doing?"

"Investigating, Mr. Hoffman," Mrs. Sperling said. "It is my vocation, much like an artist's is painting, or Mr. Stein's was this gallery. When did you get here this morning?"

"Me?" he almost yelped. "Uh, about nine or so. I went straight to the roof. Repairs, you know."

"I see."

Hoffman nervously chuckled. "Good joke."

"Joke?" Mrs. Sperling turned, then softly laughed herself. "I suppose it was a witticism, albeit unconscious."

"Yeah." Hoffman grinned without understanding.

"Well, hello, Mrs. Sperling," said a new voice from the building's back entrance.

"Sergeant Michaelson," Mrs. Sperling exclaimed warmly.

He stood just outside, with a uniformed officer behind. The sergeant was average height, good-looking in a domesticated sort of way, with soft brown receding hair, light freckles, and a medium-priced grey suit.

"You don't usually show up this soon," Michaelson continued.

"We found the body," replied Mrs. Sperling.

"That's convenient." Michaelson smiled. It was evident that these two were greater friends than rivals. Michaelson looked around. "I'm assuming that nothing's been touched or moved?"

"No. We found the body rather quickly, and I immediately put Mr. Hoffman to work phoning you. He just returned right before you arrived."

"Good." Michaelson sighed. "So, where's the body?"

"Between the tables," said Mrs. Sperling.

Michaelson looked over the scene, then followed the tracks Glen and I had made through the birdseed on the floor to between the two tables. He knelt over the body. "Let's see. We have a Caucasian male, approximately five ten in height, hundred and sixty pounds, medium brown hair. Distinct red color suggests CO poisoning. Been dead anywhere from twelve to twenty-four hours, I'm guessing. He's still in rigor. I can't tell you any more until the coroner's had a shot at him." Michaelson straightened. "Maybe you could tell me a few things."

"Such as?" Mrs. Sperling cocked her head at him curiously.

"Who is he?" Michaelson made his way along the tracks back to us.

"I believe Mr. Joshua Stein, the owner of this gallery, or at least the business." Mrs. Sperling pushed all of us into the hallway. "The building itself, I presume, is owned by Mr. Hoffman's employer."

"Hoffman?" Michaelson asked.

"Yeah, that's me." Hoffman gulped and stepped forward. "I got charge of this building."

Michaelson beckoned Hoffman to him, then got out his notebook. "Did you know Mr. Stein?"

Hoffman swallowed, then went to the space between the tables. "Yeah. That's him on the floor."

"Do you know the next of kin?"

"Uh, shit. I guess that's his wife, only they're splitting."

"They are?" asked Mrs. Sperling.

"Well, she'll know the rest of the family," Michaelson said. "How did you find the body?"

"I didn't." Hoffman pointed at Glen. "He did. He said Josh was counterfeiting."

"Glen said no such thing," interrupted Mrs. Sperling. "He didn't even complete the suggestion that we'd caught Mr. Stein in the act. I find it odd that you automatically drew that conclusion."

"Well, I..." Hoffman gulped, then hurried back to the studio doorway. "I don't know. I guess I'd heard it before. Yeah. You know, rumors and stuff. He's got the stuff here for it."

"I can think of many good reasons why a gallery owner would keep silk-screening equipment. Mr. Stein does happen to be missing drying racks, a necessary accoutrement." Mrs. Sperling pronounced that last word with a perfect French accent.

Michaelson turned to her. "Are you implying that somebody is setting this Stein up?"

"It would appear so." Mrs. Sperling indicated the hanging print. "We came down here because we needed to confront Mr. Stein about a counterfeit version of this serigraph that he sold to Glen. Mr.

Hoffman let us in, and Mr. Stein was discovered. Can you tell if he was moved after death?"

"I can't say for sure until the coroner sees him, but I'd give pretty good odds." Michaelson squatted between the tables again. "There's several squashed bird seeds around him, leaving treads. Then there's what probably killed him, namely the CO. Best way to get that is in a closed garage with a car running. I can't see any way to get a car in here. And get this. He's got a nasty knock on the back of his noggin. Had to have occurred before death. He wouldn't have that nice red color from breathing bad air otherwise."

"Therefore, an obvious indication of cold-blooded murder." Mrs. Sperling nodded sadly. "Someone banged poor Mr. Stein over the head, then left him in a closed room with an automobile running, then brought him back here. Is there any sign of the lock being forced?"

Michaelson went over and checked the door. "Nope."

"Then the killer had keys."

Hoffman's eyes widened in fear. "Shit! It was an accident! I think. It wasn't me! I was Josh's best friend."

"Mr. Hoffman," Mrs. Sperling said soothingly. "Keys can be duplicated very easily, and locks can be forced without visible outward signs. There is also the possibility that the killer gained access from Mr. Stein, himself, and used his keys. You will let me know what you find, won't you, Sergeant?"

"Naturally, Mrs. Sperling," replied Michaelson.

Mrs. Sperling ordered Eleanor forward, and Glen and I followed her back to the car.

"Where to, Mrs. Sperling?" I asked as I opened the door for her.

She gave me an address that I put it in my maps app. It was in Hollywood, on Melrose Avenue, but east of the main shopping neighborhood.

"What is this place?" asked Glen as I pulled into the traffic.

"A studio belonging to an old friend," replied Mrs. Sperling. "She's knowledgeable about counterfeiting and familiar with the current people in the racket. Perhaps she'll know who's behind our forgery."

"That's right," I said. "Those missing drying racks. But the picture was hanging. Isn't that good enough?"

"Drying racks are used in the serigraph process to dry the several copies between the application of each color," Mrs. Sperling explained.

"Well, if he's doing them one at a time," I countered.

"That's hardly economical, but possible, which is why it's not conclusive evidence of a frame, if you'll pardon the pun. I did fail to mention that the real clincher is that the picture hanging up to dry was a genuine commemorative serigraph."

"A real one?" Glen gaped. "That's totally stupid."

"I suspect the killer made a mistake," said Mrs. Sperling. "Whether or not it will be the one that catches him or her, remains to be seen."

The block where Mrs. Sperling's friend was located was lined on both sides by parked cars. I had to circle it twice to find an opening for the Lexus. Finding a parking place was easier than finding the address. It was a tacky little gallery in a block of stores trying to imitate the trendiness further west down the street.

The little shop was dusty and crowded with framed pictures stacked along the walls, and five V-shaped bins filled with Saran-Wrapped posters. Jingle bells on the door announced our arrival. As the bells died out, silence layered everything like the dust. Then, from behind a doorway curtained off by faded batik gauze, came a rustling sound. Glen started.

"Rats!" he hissed.

"In some ways," replied Mrs. Sperling.

A door slammed, wood scraped, and something fell. An elderly female voice cursed with the vehemence of a high schooler and a vocabulary that could have taught an ex-con something. More scraping and struggling, more cursing, then a soft shuffling announced the woman's arrival.

It was impossible to guess at her age beyond old. She wore her long grey hair straight and parted down the middle and wrapped with a faded red bandana headband. Her face was as wrinkled as it was tanned. A faded batik shirt covered small breasts that sagged from years without a bra. Her dirty jeans were still tight across a tiny rump. She was about average height, her eyes were bright, and she smiled as easily as she swore.

"Delilah, you old bitch!" she exclaimed with obvious delight. "What the fuck are you doing out of your capitalist nirvana?"

"Searching for information, as usual."

"As usual."

"And not about the revolution."

"As usual." The old woman rolled her eyes skyward, then peered at Mrs. Sperling. "But what? It's got to be something criminal, you old bitch. It's not like you to inquire about lawful pursuits."

"About your former life, dear."

"Which one?"

"Your current lifetime. Your former career, or more specifically, some of your old colleagues, with whom I believe you are still in touch?"

"Fuck, yes." The woman sulked. "Shit. At least, you don't make Shirley MacLaine jokes. But I've got details verified by historians. Details I have no other way of knowing."

"Yes, dear, I've seen the evidence. Interesting, but not conclusive. Still, if you'll allow me to pick your brain over lunch, we'll listen to some of your stories."

"Lunch, eh?" Her smile got even wider. "It pains me to say this, but you capitalist piss-ant bastards do know how to eat. Let me lock up."

We were on our way in minutes. Mrs. Sperling introduced us in the car. Her friend was Dolores Carmine. Whether or not that was her real name was anybody's guess. Mrs. Sperling didn't question it out loud, but I could tell she had her reservations.

I was directed west to an attractive eatery in the trendy neighborhood. The clientele was such that Dolores didn't stand out at all. Nor did Mrs. Sperling in her expensive tailored suit. The hostess seemed more amused by Eleanor than ruffled, although we did have to wait several minutes before a table large enough to accommodate her and we four humans was found.

Interrogating Dolores proved to be a delicate, time-consuming process. Her mind wandered constantly. Worse yet, Glen was fascinated by her tales of past lives. With an eager audience, there was no stopping the aging hippie.

I must admit, I found the talk interesting. I also enjoyed my fettuccine primavera. But I wondered what Mrs. Sperling wanted from Dolores Carmine. Mrs. Sperling seemed to be getting something. She dissected a grilled chicken, all the while listening intently. Every so often, between sword fights and romances on the Nile, she would ask about a different old friend of Dolores'. The reply was usually vague and led to yet another adventure.

We were all consuming white chocolate cheesecake when Mrs. Sperling asked the question that she really wanted answered.

"Dolores, among your friends in the artistic community," she began.

"Van Gogh, you mean."

"No, dear. This century, and lifetime, I might add. I know you are not engaging in any unauthorized copying, but you do have friends who are. If I were interested in work by a specific artist, could you tell me who would be involved in making copies?"

"Who the fuck do you want?"

"Hans Niedeman."

"Oh, him. Hell, lots of people in that."

"I want a good quality copy. One that could pass for the original commemorative serigraphs. It's a very high-quality ink and paper, I might add."

"Fred Gonzagos. The others, they're just shit knockoffs. But Gonzagos, he's a hell of an artist on his own. It's the White capitalist pricks who keep his work from getting recognition, so he does copies. He's the best silkscreen man in this town. No shit. You name it, he'll do it for you. He even did a few lost Renoirs last summer for some tourists."

"So, he's adept at lithographs and oils."

"Right down to the fuckin' signatures and numbers. He'll be a hard bird to catch. Real spooky. And, Delilah, you know I won't testify."

"I have no intention of asking you."

"What do you want him for?"

"I believe I may possess some of his work."

"Delilah, you bitch, that ain't all."

Mrs. Sperling sighed. "Dolores, I can't afford to let you scare him away. You must understand, I have no reason to suspect him, but he may be able to shed some light on a rather nasty murder in Beverly Hills. It does involve his work. You might suggest that a disappearance could make him look very bad."

"Anybody but you." Dolores shook her head. "It could be just racist bullshit again. But… Fuck, I wouldn't have mentioned his name if I didn't think you'd give him every chance. I'm counting on you."

"I'm only interested in the truth."

"You and the Tooth Fairy. Fred's an okay guy. But this murder shit worries me. Just between us, I say he could be guilty. Most bastards who make copies are pacifists. Pricks, but non-violent. Fred usually is, too, except when he's drunk. I don't invite him to parties, and a lot of people I know won't either. He wrecks too much. Fuckin' near killed Tancy Greer last week."

"Then I would say it's not likely Mr. Gonzagos is behind this. It was definitely pre-meditated." Mrs. Sperling dug through her purse. "Glen, will you summon the waiter? It's time to settle the account."

As soon as the tab was settled, we returned Dolores to her gallery. I pulled out, then stopped for a red light at the end of the block.

"Well, now what?" asked Glen.

"Donna, did you hear the address Dolores gave me?" Mrs. Sperling countered.

"Yes, I did." I'd already put it in the maps app.

"We're going to talk to this Gonzagos dude?" Glen gulped.

"You needn't be so nervous, Glen," said Mrs. Sperling. "I did say that the evidence points away from him."

"We'll just hope he's not drunk," I teased over a voice telling me to turn left in 1,000 feet.

"If he is intoxicated, we'll merely beat a hasty retreat," Mrs. Sperling replied to Glen's groan. "In vino is not necessarily veritas."

"Oh." Glen frowned. He had no idea what Mrs. Sperling meant, but he wasn't about to admit it.

Fred Gonzagos' place was in the Fairfax district. It was an apartment in a larger house with a pink stucco Spanish exterior and a black wrought iron staircase sweeping up to his door. The building had probably been built in the thirties. The neighborhood was quite neat and almost sleepy.

Mrs. Sperling decided to stay in the car. I guess she didn't expect much success. I felt brave, so I left Glen with her, and went to the door myself. Mrs. Sperling was right. I got no answer, at least not from the apartment.

"Hey! Who are you?" called a matronly voice with a thick Spanish accent below me.

I cautiously came down the stairs. "Um, I'm looking for Mr. Gonzagos. I understand he has some Niedemans for sale."

"I don't give a damn what you here for," growled the woman, a stout Hispanic lady whose age and bearing matched her voice. "I want to know who you are."

"I'm a customer for Mr. Gonzagos." I remained firm.

She threw up her arms. "Well, you can't talk to him. He's been out of town since yesterday. And don't get no fancy ideas. This whole house got more alarms than the White House, and they're all connected to the police station."

"I believe you." I backed off. "Any idea when he'll be back?"

"Few days, few weeks, who knows?"

"Know where he went?"

"If I knew that, I know when he come back!" She waddled back into her abode, grumbling under her breath in Spanish.

"Well?" asked Glen upon my return.

"A big fat zip," I grumbled. "He's out of town

since yesterday, which sounds kind of suspicious to me."

"It does," agreed Mrs. Sperling. "Any return date or location?"

"None."

"Even more suspicious, but not at all likely to stand up in court. Could be a very convenient coincidence for the real killer."

"Where to now, Mrs. Sperling?" I asked, starting the engine.

"Home," she answered. "I do have a life outside of counterfeit serigraphs and murders, and you, Donna, have some moving to do."

"That's right. Will I need any towels or anything like that?"

"Just your personal toiletries. Do you think you'll be able to return by six? I'd like to let Mrs. Osgood know how many to expect for dinner."

"I don't know. I'll just hit a drive-thru."

"Ooph! I'll ask Mrs. Osgood to save you a plate."

"Thanks."

The first thing I did when we got back to the house was call my mother. She was thrilled to hear I was well and truly employed and moving out. I found out how thrilled when I got home. She had called Dad home early from their store and had him dismantling my bed by the time I got there.

"My room is already furnished, Mom," I told her. "I thought I said so on the phone."

"I know, dear. But we're turning this one into a study. Dad's computer is going in here, and my desk. I don't know, Walt. What do you think of mauve?"

"It's okay," grunted my father, struggling with the box springs.

"Walt, are you even listening to me? I'm trying to make a decision here, and I need your help."

Smiling to myself, I went and got the suitcases my mom was letting me borrow. I doubted Mom would get any help from my dad. As much as I love him, I must admit I've never heard him give an opinion on anything. I packed quickly.

As I left, Mom grabbed her purse and followed me out the door.

"Where are you going?" I asked.

"To the paint store. I've got an appointment with the decorator there."

"So much for empty nest syndrome."

"Oh, Donna." Mom sighed as she stopped and looked at me. "You're not hurt, are you?"

I shrugged. "I don't know. I know you've had plans for my room for a while."

"Well, your brother and sisters are gone. I guess I've been so used to you being gone so much, it felt like you didn't live here. That, and I've already been through the separation process. You know how bad I felt when Debbie left. Of course, she was my baby."

"And going to live with her boyfriend."

"At least they got married last year. What a mess that was. I think that's why I'm acting like this. Get it over with right away. Short and sweet." She suddenly hugged me. "My firstborn angel. I'm gonna miss you."

"I can stay," I teased.

"Hell, no! Oh, Donna! You know what I mean. I'm serious, darling. If this doesn't work out, you come right on back. I don't want you to be afraid of that. You're always welcome here. I said that to Peter, and Denise, and Debbie. I'm still saying that to Debbie."

"You are never going to forgive Ernie, are you?"

"She was only eighteen, and he was nineteen. How were they supposed to support themselves?"

"Well, they did, and still are, better than I was for a long time."

"That's different, dear. Maybe your father didn't understand, but I knew there are just some things you have to get out of your system."

"Yeah." I sighed to myself.

"Now, are you gonna be alright?"

"Oh, sure. Mrs. Sperling is a perfect lady." With a penchant for murder. But I wasn't about to tell my mother that.

"At least she isn't a man. I am a little worried, but you know best. Why don't you come home Sunday for dinner? Peter and Elise are coming, and Denise said she might show."

"If Mrs. Sperling doesn't need me to take her somewhere."

"Call me, then. Oops! I'd better get running. Take care, darling."

"You, too, Mom."

I kissed her, then got back into my old Altima,

and headed west to Los Angeles and my new life. I couldn't help sighing. While I didn't dare admit it to my mother, or Mrs. Sperling, I still hadn't gotten the show business thing out of my system. I found myself wondering how long it would take to save up for new pictures, and whether I could get a night or two off for classes, or maybe an afternoon or morning to go to auditions.

The dream of making it was still as strong as ever. I doubted I'd ever be rid of it. But one thing my folks always taught me was that if you make a commitment, you don't break it. I had promised I'd be self-supporting when I turned twenty-six, and at last, I was.

Well, I had moved out at any rate. My new home was a fair-sized room, decorated with a Louis Quinze escritoire and chair, a matching dresser, lush rose-colored carpeting, and a simple bed covered by a tapestry style bedspread featuring lords and ladies being pastoral in eighteenth-century dress. The walls were bare to allow me my own tastes. A full-length mirror was bolted to the closet door. The closet was huge and had plenty of extra shelves built in.

The only drawback to the whole set-up was that I had to share a bathroom with Glen. Upon the departure of my predecessor, he had spread out. The counter was littered with mousse cans, gel tubes, blow dryer, soaps, creams, shaving equipment, aspirin bottles, tissues, nasal decongestants, and nameless other containers. Stuck to the mirror were pictures of various art, mostly women. The bathtub/shower had its share of bottles and several hangers with drying sweaters and pants hanging from the curtain rod.

It was a pity the room was such a mess. It would have been a gorgeous bathroom otherwise. The tub and counter were both black marble. The cabinets were lovely white French Provincial, and the fixtures were bright brass with white porcelain. The counter, fortunately, had two sinks. The linens were lush soft towels in grey, navy, and white, and were laying on the floor.

I picked one up.

"Oh, you're back," said Glen, as he came in.

"Yeah." I looked at him. "You are worse than my brother and two sisters combined."

"I, uh, gotta clean up. Set your stuff down here and go eat dinner. The plate's in the oven, salad in the refrigerator. No feeding Eleanor."

"Okay."

I wandered through the house until I found the kitchen. The lights were on, and a large Black woman dressed in a white uniform and apron bent over something on the stove. She looked up and smiled when she saw me.

"You must be Donna," she said with a slight Jamaican rhythm. "I'm Mrs. Osgood. I cook for Mrs. Sperling. The dinner is in the oven. Help yourself."

"Thanks." I retrieved the plate and got the salad out of the refrigerator. I was almost afraid to eat, the plate looked so lovely. There were two lamb cutlets, perfectly pink, browned swirled potatoes, and carrots and zucchini that were just starting to lose their bright color from the wait in the oven. "You do this every night?"

"Not always lamb. I cook many other things."

"But so fancy."

She let out a big, well-rounded laugh. "I am trained at the Cordon Bleu in Paris. I have been a cook at many of the best restaurants in Los Angeles. But I did not like it. I work for Mrs. Sperling and do things like this. You see? A beautiful demi-glace. This one must wait overnight for the full flavor to come out. You cannot always do this at a restaurant. There it is always fast, and good cooking will not always take that." She breathed in the steam coming from the pot and sighed in pure pleasure.

She finished up while I ate and left. I continued my meal, browsing through the mail I had brought from home. It was all ads, and my Backstage Magazine. I spread the trade paper out and forced myself to read the front of it before skipping to the casting notices. I heard soft clicking, then saw Eleanor morosely look up at me.

"I'm not supposed to feed you," I told her.

The dog whined, then padded over to the refrigerator. I went back to dinner and reading.

About five minutes later, I became aware of hot breath on my hand.

"Eleanor! Get down!" Mrs. Sperling's well-bred voice commanded.

Eleanor removed her paws from the tabletop and slunk over to her corner by the refrigerator. Mrs. Sperling stood in the doorway.

"How..." I stopped myself from asking the rude question with a great deal of stammering. "Oh, uh, hi."

"Enjoying your meal?" Mrs. Sperling headed for the pantry with her own exquisite grace.

"Yeah. It's terrific. Mrs. Osgood informed me that you always eat this well."

"When I'm here, I do." She opened the pantry door, reached in, then frowned. "Unfortunately, Mrs. Osgood considers the kitchen her domain, which makes it a little awkward for me when I want a snack after she goes home." She pulled out a box of powdered milk and sniffed at it. "Are these my biscuits? No." She rummaged again. "Ah. These. Arrowroot biscuits. One of my greater weaknesses. Now, if she just hasn't moved the milk."

She negotiated the refrigerator door and Eleanor and rescued the carton of low fat.

"Are you all moved in?" she asked, sitting down with a glass, the milk and cookie box.

"Not completely. I still have some clothes and books and odds and ends at my folks' place. I'll be retrieving them as time goes on."

"That's convenient."

"Umm." I looked her over carefully. "I don't know if this is too personal to ask..."

"But you'd like to know why I'm investigating a murder when I am obviously not a member of the police department." Mrs. Sperling smiled, completely unruffled by my nosiness. "Given that I have you assisting me, you certainly have a right to know. I'm a private investigator, by avocation. I have a license just for credibility's sake, and I occasionally accept fees."

"Oh." I frowned. "But this morning, we were only going to find out about the forgery, then you went ahead after the murderer. Aren't you supposed to have a client before you do that?"

"Well..." Mrs. Sperling let out a lady-like, but merry giggle. "It's only a matter of finding one. I'll admit, it's a rather backward way to go about it, but it works. Glen has agreed to act as my client for the time being. There is another who might be more interested, but he, alas, is not home. By the way, Glen usually screens my calls, but you may answer the phone, also. Leave any messages for me on the voice recorder next to the hall phone. You might also want to write them down just in case."

"Sure." I went back to eating. "Have you heard any more on the Stein murder?"

"Not much. Sergeant Michaelson questioned Mr. Hoffman more extensively than I did. Mr. Hoffman claims he worked late because of the power outage, then went out with friends, the latter part of which the good sergeant has already verified. Mr. Hoffman's landlady confirms that Mr. Hoffman came in when he did, and says he got up at his usual time of seven o'clock. At least she heard his clock radio go off. According to the sergeant, she rather belabored that point. Apparently, Mr. Hoffman is in the habit of turning the volume on quite loud and forgetting to turn the thing off. She lives under him."

"I guess Hoffman's out, then."

"Not necessarily. I have too few facts to begin ruling out suspects. Still, it doesn't seem likely that Mr. Hoffman is the killer. He didn't strike me as being terribly intelligent, and this murder was quite cleverly put together. Perhaps not the murder itself, but the way the body was left..." Mrs. Sperling slowly froze as she became immersed in her thoughts.

I didn't really notice. "Maybe it was Gonzagos, then. Maybe he blew his stack and hit Stein, then took advantage of it and left him in the car."

"It doesn't really fit what we know of Mr. Gonzagos psychologically. He is only violent when he's drunk, and inebriated, he could never have set up the body that way. Still, it would give him access to Mr. Stein's keys, which were not found, by the way." Mrs. Sperling snapped out of her daze and went back to dunking cookies in milk. "It's far too soon to say for sure. The counterfeiting motive is an awkward one, as it is an obvious attempt to discredit Mr. Stein. Furthermore, despite his suspicious disappearance, we cannot say anything definite about Mr. Gonzagos psychologically until we've met him. Dolores is extremely accurate in her perceptions of people, but one can misconstrue motives."

I grinned. "How'd you get into investigating? I mean, well..."

"That my blindness would seem to be an insurmountable handicap in the detection field?" She laughed. "It can be a problem if I can't get accurate detailed descriptions. But a lot of detection is understanding the psychology of the criminal. The rest is merely applying logic. Even the most unbalanced and insane behave to a logic of their own. The trick is in discovering it."

"That's some trick."

"One merely adds up the discrepancies, and there's always a logical reason for them."

"But still..."

"Everyone makes the art of deduction harder than it is. You deduce things every day."

"How?"

She smiled. "Well, you look out your window in the morning. Your room is quite nice and warm. But outside the sky is overcast. What do you do?"

"Put on a coat when I go outside because it's cold."

"But what if it's June?"

I laughed. "I'd put on my shorts. The clouds will have burnt off by one."

"Brava! You made a deduction based on clues. Because I have no sight, I must rely on other clues than you and make more deductions just to survive on my own. Maybe that's why I'm such a good detective. I also tend towards an orderly mindset."

"And you just started snooping one day."

"Not really. My father used to read to me quite copiously when I was young, there not being nearly as many audiobooks available that there are now. He was always a fan of detective fiction, Rex

Stout and Raymond Chandler being his favorites. They weren't mine. I didn't have any sympathy for the characters, and I always guessed who the bad guy was long before Father did. Then Father read Whose Body? to me, by Dorothy Sayers. I've been an incurable Lord Peter Wimsey fan ever since. I still figured them out rather quickly, but at least I had sympathy for the characters, and for detecting. In my innocence, I decided that if Nero Wolfe could get away with never seeing the scene, so could I, and without being a pompous old poop about it." She sucked on a milk-soaked cookie before eating it. "It was terribly juvenile, but I was determined to prove that I could do it, which I did."

"But why keep on, especially if you've made your point? Unless you need to for a living."

"My living was made for me years ago." She chuckled and soaked another cookie. "I keep on for the same reason actors continue to act after they've made their fortunes or CEOs continue to go into the office when they could comfortably retire. You're not going to stop dancing when you've made your fortune."

"Well, no. Not that it's likely I'll get my chance."

"Either way, you'll still dance. It's what you are. And I am a detective. I can't stop any more than you can."

"Hm." I looked at her carefully. "Do you resent being blind?"

"No. I've never seen, so I don't really know what I'm supposedly missing. I don't know that life is that much harder. I'd like to drive myself, perhaps. But even when I didn't have a chauffeur, I always found public transportation to be sufficient."

"It wasn't too limiting?"

"Occasionally. Life is full of limits. There are some things that you simply cannot do. But do you spend much time grieving over it?"

"No."

"Neither do I." Her smile grew soft. "I did resent being different as a child. However, given the perspective of time, I realize that I would have still been different even with sight. My parents are unusual people. They believe in convention only so far as it prevents anarchy. My father always said to stay on the right side of the law but live on your own terms. He and my mother truly do."

"Are they retired?"

"More or less. My father spends about four months out of the year overseeing his business interests. The rest of the time, he and my mother travel."

"Lucky stiffs."

"They're extremely lucky, mostly because they're blessed with the ability to be happy wherever they are, and they're hopelessly in love with each other."

"That's great." This time I heard Eleanor at the same time as Mrs. Sperling. "Hey!"

"Eleanor, to your room," commanded Mrs. Sperling.

Sulking, Eleanor padded out.

"How long have you had her?" I asked.

"Three years now."

"Did the guide dog school name her Eleanor, or was that your idea?"

She chuckled. "Mine. I changed it the third day I had her. It seemed more appropriate. Her full name is Eleanor Roosevelt."

"I don't get it."

"She's such a buttinsky."

"Ah. You're a Republican."

"My father is and used to be vehemently so. My mother is a devout Democrat, a fact she's hidden from my father all their lives. She comes from a time when women catered to their men, not that she ever did. She merely thinks that they have such a nice relationship, why muck it up with nonessentials?" She stood. "I'd best get back upstairs. I have a recording to make for a friend of mine. Just leave your dish in the sink. Help yourself to breakfast."

"Thanks. Um. What time will you be needing me tomorrow?"

"Eleven, at the earliest."

"Good. There's a dance class in Hollywood that I usually take. It goes from eight to ten. I'd kind of like to keep it up when it doesn't interfere. I don't want to get out of shape."

"Especially if a good role comes up."

"Uh, yeah." I sighed. "But this job comes first."

"I understand. You're a dancer. Do you still have an agent?"

"A commercial one. My theatrical agent I'm

dropping. He almost never sends me out."

"Too bad for him." She put the milk back in the refrigerator, then paused. "Donna, if you do get an audition or job, please tell me. I'm willing to work around things."

"You are? Aren't you afraid I'll get too tied up in it?"

"Not if we're communicating. And although I'm confident you are very talented, I also know the odds. Even with a great deal of talent, innocents like you have a harder time making it than others. I seriously doubt there will be that many conflicts. But keep trying, Donna."

"Thanks," I muttered, utterly surprised, and awed by her generosity.

left the house the next morning with an apple and a piece of toast in hand. All was silent. I got back at ten-thirty and didn't see anyone on the way to the shower. I was out and dressed by eleven. Wondering what to do, I wandered into the living room, then the kitchen.

Mrs. Sperling was enjoying either a late breakfast or an early lunch. Mrs. Osgood took something sweet and spicy smelling from the oven.

"Good morning, Donna," said Mrs. Sperling without turning to me. "Did your class go well?"

"Pretty good. I'm a little stiff. I haven't worked out in three days."

"Do you like ginger snaps?" Mrs. Osgood asked, smiling.

"Sure," I replied.

"Please sit down and join me," said Mrs. Sperling. "You're probably quite hungry."

"Based on what clues?" I teased, sitting down.

"You were just strenuously exercising, which also means you ate very little before your class if anything at all." With only one false start, she located an empty plate on the table and filled it.

"We're indulging in red meat for brunch today. Steak and scrambled eggs with mushroom sauce, grilled potatoes, and green peas. Mrs. Osgood takes very good care of us and makes sure we get the really fattening stuff early in the day, so we can work it off."

"Thanks. Not so much, please. I'm not a heavy eater any time of the day."

"Do you drink water or milk?" asked Mrs. Osgood, placing a glass and silver next to my hand.

"Milk's fine. Thanks."

"Ah, another fighter against the scourge of osteoporosis," observed Mrs. Sperling.

"Not really," I answered. "I just like milk. I'm glad you have low fat. I can't stand milk you can see through."

"Nor can I abide the taste of nonfat. I have tried and tried, and I still don't like it."

I chuckled in agreement. "So. What's up today? You said you needed me at eleven."

"I said that would be the earliest. There's a young girl I'm tutoring at the Braille Institute. She called and said she was sick today and couldn't make it. I suspect she hasn't got her homework done again. But alas, I have no evidence. Nonetheless, it is a fortunate cancellation. We shall finish our meal at leisure, then call on Sergeant Michaelson."

"Do you have an appointment?"

"No."

"But what if he's not there?"

"All the better. We shall be able to read the

reports without his bias."

Sergeant Michaelson was on his lunch break when we arrived at the Beverly Hills Police Station.

"Mrs. Sperling, those reports have not been released to the general public," sighed a smallish clerk in a uniform. His nameplate said Bradley.

"Since when am I the general public?" Mrs. Sperling countered.

"I know, but..."

"Must I bother Chief Matthews?"

Bradley threw his arms in the air and searched through a file cabinet.

"You're lucky he's your cousin," he said, handing her a file folder.

"I'm even luckier he owed me one." Mrs. Sperling smiled and handed the file to me.

I waited until Bradley had left the room. "What did the chief owe you?"

"A major case, and his life. He wanted to give me a medal and the substantial reward that was being offered. I asked for free access to all Beverly Hills police reports, past, present and future, and got it. He suggested he would rue the day, but he has yet to. By the way, I am counting on your complete discretion."

"Nary a word, ma'am." I opened the file. "Let's see. We've got photographs of the room. There are some suitcases under the cot. I don't think I mentioned that."

"No. How interesting. Mr. Hoffman mentioned that Mr. Stein and his wife are newly separated. I suspect Mr. Stein was living in his gallery. Were the contents inventoried?"

"Uh, yeah. Here they are. Twelve shirts, nine pairs of pants, thirty-one pairs of briefs..."

"Hm. Obsessive about clean underwear. Go on."

"Twelve pairs of socks, four belts, eight sets of suspenders, seven tank tops, nine t-shirts, eight pairs of jeans..."

"How many suitcases were there?"

"Three. Um, two bathrobes, one pair of slippers, and eight pairs of shoes."

"That's everything?"

"Yeah. They didn't list colors."

"No pajamas."

"Nope."

"That's interesting."

"He probably slept in the raw," I said and looked over the report again. "I don't see any toiletries listed either. There was some soap, toothpaste, and a toothbrush in the bathroom, but nothing else. He should at least have shampoo and deodorant, more likely he'd have everything that Glen has spread out all over the bathroom."

"Odd. Glen is an excellent housekeeper."

"Not in the bathroom. It's clean and all. There's just lots of clutter."

"Oh. As for the late Mr. Stein, I take it there is no shower in the gallery."

"You take it correct."

"Then no toiletries. I would venture to guess that Mr. Stein is a member of a gymnasium in the local area, and has a permanent locker there, and that is where his toiletries are."

"Of course."

"We should verify that. If the toiletries are indeed missing, that could be an important clue, and their actual location an even better one. What else does the report say?"

"It just describes the room, and our statements, and the conversation with Mr. Hoffman, and Bedelia Parrish, his landlady."

"It's early, yet, but there wouldn't happen to be a coroner's report, would there?"

"Yeah, here. He died between eight-thirty p.m. and two a.m. He received a blow on the head, in the back, close to the time of death. It was definitely carbon monoxide poisoning. The body had been moved since death. Stomach contents were potatoes, ketchup, mustard, pickles, reconstituted onions, hamburger, bread, cola."

"Oh, the poor man! Fast food for a last meal." Mrs. Sperling shuddered.

I grinned. "He'd eaten two to four hours before he died. He'd had at least one hernia operation, probably as a child, and apparently no other surgeries. There was a long scar on his leg, a cut sewn together, also fairly old. No signs of needle marks or other illegal drugs, beyond some scarring in the lungs typical of moderate marijuana use."

"Has he been formally identified?"

"Yes, by his wife, Ramona Bistler."

"Ramona Bistler? No wonder they were splitting." Mrs. Sperling frowned. "That was a terribly catty thing to say. But unfortunately, apt."

"You know her?"

"Not well. A friend of a friend. I've met her at several parties. Her husband was never with her, nor did she tend towards fidelity, I'm sorry to say. I have eyewitnesses on that account."

"Hm. Well, the lab report confirms everything else we know. Oh, there's a note here that the print in the room is being authenticated."

"And I just got a call before lunch that it's genuine." Sergeant Michaelson's voice startled me. "Dear Mrs. Sperling, taking advantage of the Chief's graciousness again, I see."

"Blood tells, dear Sergeant." Mrs. Sperling smiled primly.

"And what conclusions have you drawn?"

"None yet, except that Mr. Stein was slightly obsessive about underwear. You didn't happen to go through it, did you?"

"As a matter of fact, I did. So?"

"Was it in good repair?"

"It all looked brand new to me. Come to think of it, I thought he'd been saving it over the years. It was a lot of underwear. But I didn't see any signs of wear."

"Ah. A very orderly, clean person, wouldn't you say?"

"Yeah. His desk was in pretty good shape."

"Then why was there bird seed all over the place?"

"That's easy," I put in. "Birds are a mess."

"But all over the room?" Mrs. Sperling frowned.

"Usually, the mess is somewhat contained."

I shrugged. "It blew around. My sister had birdseed all the way to the bathroom when she had a bird."

"But is your sister neat and orderly? Mr. Stein was." She thought about it, then brushed it off. "Well, that piece of the puzzle shall eventually fit. Is there anything else in the report, Donna?"

"Not that I can see."

"Anything to add, Sergeant?"

He grinned. "As a matter of fact, yes. A couple salespeople from two different shops in the neighborhood said that on Wednesday they saw Stein arguing with a customer. It was pretty loud, and a piece of pottery got broken. One of the witnesses identified the customer as Devon of Devonaire. Does that ring a bell?"

"No," replied Mrs. Sperling.

"There's a store on Melrose called Devonaire," I said. "It's women's clothing."

Michaelson shrugged. "I think somebody said the guy is a clothing designer."

"That's very interesting," Mrs. Sperling said. "We'll have to talk to him about it."

"That's all I've got for you," Sergeant Michaelson said.

"Fine. We shall vacate, then. Oh, one thing more, Sergeant. The officer patrolling the neighborhood of the gallery. Did he happen to note the presence of any cars in that alley that night?"

"Officer Willoughby was on duty and, uh,

made no such notation." Sergeant Michaelson shifted.

"You have reason to doubt the officer?" Mrs. Sperling had caught his unease also.

"Not per se. The local security patrol didn't note any suspicious vehicles either. Willoughby just gives me a bad feeling is all."

"I see. Perhaps we should press Officer Willoughby on this matter. If you would be so good as to give me his address, I will do so."

"I'll go you one better. Here he is right now."

Officer Willoughby was a young man with blonde hair. Tall and slightly filled out, he was wearing a worn polo shirt and faded jeans. Sergeant Michaelson waved him into the detectives' room.

"Yeah, Sergeant. What's up?" Willoughby growled passively.

"This is Mrs. Delilah Sperling," answered the sergeant. "She's taken an interest in the Stein murder."

"You're off duty," Mrs. Sperling said.

"Uh, yeah." Willoughby looked puzzled. I, too, wondered how Mrs. Sperling had figured that one out.

"If I remember correctly, your shift should end at six thirty in the morning," Mrs. Sperling said to the unasked question. "What brings you here at this time of day?"

"Got a friend on the cross-over shift. We're gonna play racquetball when he gets off."

"Ah. I see. I understand you were patrolling

the alley and neighborhood around Mr. Stein's gallery the night before last."

"Sure."

"And you did not notice any suspicious cars?"

"No."

"None?"

"None."

"Odd."

"I don't know what anyone else is saying, ma'am. But I did not see anything out of place in that alley all night."

"Very well, then." Mrs. Sperling rewarded him with a smile. She signaled me, and we bade good-bye to the two policemen and left the station.

We headed back to the gallery. Mrs. Sperling wanted to find out some more about Mr. Stein's psychology. Most of the people in the neighboring stores knew him, but nobody knew him very well.

"He was one of those loner types," sighed Geraldine, the owner of the clothes boutique in the buildling next to the gallery. "He was real nice. And responsible, too. Always showed up at our merchants' association meetings. On time, which is more than I can say. He always said hi when he saw me. But I can't say I knew him. Hell, I didn't even know he was married until I heard about the split." She sniffed. "I'm gonna miss him. He was a real hot dresser. Really had style, not like some guys you see, all trendy and no panache. Or worse yet, complete rebellion. Poor Josh. He really knew how to dress."

Geraldine was the most expansive on Mr. Josh

Stein's personality. Most of the other merchants muttered platitudes about Mr. Stein's nice nature, and that was it. Until we met Mr. Leon Dresser.

He was one of the salespeople Sergeant Michaelson had mentioned. Dressed in a bright blue jumpsuit and beret, he was an average sized man with cropped blond hair, and earrings parading all along the edges of his ears.

"Oh, who knows what they were arguing about!" he gushed. "I certainly didn't care. Devon is about as obnoxious as they come. He thinks he's the only person with taste on the entire West Coast. Have you seen his stuff? I've seen better on the beds in the Sears catalog. Of course, I was surprised. Shocked, even. I mean Josh, well it took a lot to get him mad, if you know what I mean. But there they were, yelling at each other. Then the pottery went, I'm not sure how, and Josh lost it. That's when I left. Seeing a man lose his temper like that is not a pretty sight, nor one for strangers."

Mrs. Sperling agreed with a sigh.

"Kind of suspicious, huh?" I said as we walked to the gallery and the car.

"Not necessarily," replied Mrs. Sperling. "We shall have to wait and see if the argument is significant. Eleanor, halt. This is the alley?"

"Yeah."

"Anyplace near the gallery that a car could hide?"

"Not really. There's a large metal trash bin two doors down. But that would only hide a small car, and from this end only. There's a major cross street a block down."

"The car could have come and gone between both patrols. It wouldn't have needed to stay long."

"Five minutes, max. So now what?"

"That's a good question. I recommend home for the moment. We must find where Mr. Stein's gymnasium is. I've a feeling we shall have to find that out from Ms. Ramona Bistler, and that will require strategy. Yes, home is definitely the place."

"Right away, Mrs. Sperling."

As I drove into the driveway, Glen pulled in behind us and whipped around to the other end of the drive. I let Mrs. Sperling out near the kitchen door, then garaged the Lexus. I had to chuckle as I looked at the driveway. At one end was the garage which sheltered Mrs. Sperling's bright red V.W. Bug convertible, the later one they made, and the black Mercedes CSL that she used as her limousine, in addition to the Lexus. Along the side of the garage were parked my Altima, Glen's beat-up Toyota sedan, and a Triumph Spitfire that belonged to Mrs. Osgood. The three older cars looked as though they were huddling together, bemoaning their derelict appearances amongst so much wealth.

Inside, Glen tried to get information out of Mrs. Sperling.

"You mean you have no idea?" he groaned.

"I have some, but it's much too early to form a hypothesis. There are many more facts to be gathered first."

"Bitchen," he sulked. Mrs. Sperling cleared her throat. "Oh, sorry. Nobody else thinks it's a cuss word."

"Nonetheless, it's insulting to female dogs."

"Yeah." Glen sighed. "I guess what I really want to know is how am I going to get my real Niedeman?"

"That is something the lawyers will have to decide," Mrs. Sperling replied. "I'd best warn you, you may not."

Glen held back a barrage of profanities. "That's all I need. I'm already out several hundred dollars, if I can even find one."

"I'm sorry, Glen." Mrs. Sperling was genuinely so. "But don't panic yet. A lot depends on how involved Mr. Stein was in the counterfeiting business. If there are criminal charges against him, the court may put a lien on his estate. It might also see that you are recompensed. It all depends on how the questions are answered, and how you present your case."

The doorbell rang and Glen hurried off to answer it. I followed Mrs. Sperling into the living room. Glen arrived with us.

"It's Mrs. Delgado," he said. "Are you receiving?"

Mrs. Sperling perked up. "Norma? Of course, I will. Show her in."

Glen left.

"Um, should I excuse myself?" I asked.

"Not unless you want to."

Mrs. Sperling turned to greet her guest. Norma

Delgado was probably around Mrs. Sperling's age, and easily as well kept up. Her black hair showed slivers of grey and was drawn into a neat bun at the back of her neck. She was shorter and rounder than Mrs. Sperling. Her shirtwaist dress was a polished cotton with the kind of detailed tailoring that meant money.

"Delilah, I just happened to be in the neighborhood, and I thought I'd take a chance and see if you were in," she said with sincere warmth. Just a hint of an accent belied her Hispanic ancestry.

"We're fortunate, then," replied Mrs. Sperling. "I just got back. Please have a seat."

"Thank you." Mrs. Delgado smiled at me. "Is this a new friend or employee?"

"Oh, this is Donna Brechter, my new chauffeur. Donna, this is Mrs. Norma Delgado."

"Pleased to meet you," I replied with a quick nod.

"Go ahead and sit down, Donna," Mrs. Sperling directed.

I sat down on the edge of the sofa.

"What happened to Jimmy?" Mrs. Delgado asked.

"He sold too many books," said Mrs. Sperling. "His publisher sent him on a publicity tour, and he had to leave before I could get another chauffeur. He felt very bad about it, in fact, I had quite a time convincing him he should go. I survived with taxis in the meantime, and Glen, when he wasn't in class. But now I have Donna, and she's been most satisfactory."

"Thanks," I muttered and blushed.

"Good." Mrs. Delgado smiled again. "Actually, I was going to call you. Have you heard about Ramona Bistler's husband?"

"Oh, yes." A mischievous smile crept onto Mrs. Sperling's lips.

"Oh, no. When I heard he'd been murdered, I had this strange feeling you'd be up to your elbows in it, or about to be." Mrs. Delgado looked Mrs. Sperling over. "Well, am I wrong?"

"Very right, I'm afraid. We found the body."

"And have been investigating ever since. Then maybe you will be interested. Alisa Montrose is having a party tonight, after the viewing."

"I'm not sure..."

"I know Alisa is unbearable, and frankly, I don't blame you. But the party is for Ramona, to cheer her up, not that... Oh dear, I can't help it. Not that Ramona needs it."

Mrs. Sperling sighed. "I'm afraid Ramona does ask for a certain amount of talk behind her back."

"I know. But I hate being catty. It's bad enough having to be pleasant to people like Alisa Montrose. I don't want to be like her. I'm serious. If it weren't for Mario depending on her vote, and everyone else's, I'd make it a point to avoid her."

"Such is the burden of a politician's wife. And how is the judge?"

"Working like a dog, as usual. He's beginning to worry about being re-elected. Then there's all the work he must do as his job. I say he's crazy, but he loves it, so I'm happy for him. Fortunately, my business keeps me occupied when I want to be. Oh, Mario said to invite you to dinner next week. He wants to talk to somebody without campaigning."

"Certainly. Is Friday good?"

"Perfect. As for tonight, the viewing is from six to eight, party from eight-thirty to whenever. I don't mean to scare you off, but Alisa specifically asked me to invite you. I think it's ghoulish curiosity. Still, I thought that if you were looking into the matter, it would provide you with an opportunity to talk to Ramona."

"It would indeed." Mrs. Sperling lapsed into a brief daze. She snapped out of it quickly. "I suppose I shall suffer through it. I take it you'll be there also?"

"Of course. I'm going to be partying from now until the election next June. I've got to do my bit to keep Mario on his bench."

"Let me know what parties you'll be going to, and I'll try and fit a few into my schedule."

"Delilah, you are a doll." Mrs. Delgado got up. "Masochistic, but a doll. I'm going to hurry on now. I'll see you tonight. Don't get up. I'll see myself out."

"Donna," Mrs. Sperling said when we were alone. "I don't think I'll be needing you for the rest of the afternoon. But have the Mercedes ready at eight-fifteen."

"Oh. Okay."

"Did you have plans for tonight?"

"Strictly tentative."

"Well, unless they're early, don't cancel them. I doubt I'll be late."

"You don't have to do that. I don't mind working."

"I'm sure you don't, and normally I wouldn't. But I seriously doubt I'm going to be spending much time at Alisa Montrose's."

I spent that afternoon reading. Around six I took the Mercedes out to see if it needed gas. The tank was half full. I went ahead and filled it the rest of the way. At seven-thirty I got dressed and braided my hair. I didn't have a uniform. Mrs. Sperling had told me I wouldn't need one. I still felt I had to look something like the part. Besides, I had a plan.

"I do hope you will keep your ears open while we're at the party," Mrs. Sperling said on the way over. "Hired help is notorious for gossiping, and you never know when you might pick up an interesting tidbit."

"No problem," I answered. "Maybe we ought to set up some sort of signal in case I catch something hot."

"I was about to suggest that. Your predecessor used to whistle."

"I can do that. I'm something of a virtuoso." I snickered with pride.

"Mozart, Symphony Number Forty, in G Minor."

"Uh, which one's that?"

Mrs. Sperling whistled from the first movement.

"That one." I started whistling along.

After a few bars, Mrs. Sperling dropped out and just listened.

"I'm impressed," she said.

"I have a weakness for Mozart," I confessed.

"That's a blessing. All Jimmy could manage was 'Take Me Out to the Ballgame.' I enjoy Mozart, although Beethoven is my weakness."

"Really? Do you just listen to classical music?"

"Heavens, no. Glen recently introduced me to Beyonce and JayZ. I also like Glen Miller, Ray Charles, the Beatles, Wagner, Lady Gaga, Beach Boys, Katy Perry, some Van Halen, Benny Goodman..."

"And the list goes on. That's quite a combination."

"I have very eclectic tastes, and I make a point of keeping up on what's current in the popular arts, as well as the more esoteric ones. My father always encouraged me to try new things. He was the only adult I knew who liked rock and roll when I was young."

"I hope I stay that young. Looks like we're here. Why don't you stay put when I stop, and I'll strut out all the hot stuff I learned in chauffeur school."

Mrs. Sperling chuckled. "Most certainly. I love a good entrance."

Eleanor was the first out of the car. Mrs. Sperling first tested for the curb with her foot, a movement so smooth I barely noticed it. As she stood, she stumbled and caught my shoulder.

"You okay?" I asked as she righted herself.

"Perfectly all right. Give me an hour, then you can go dancing with your friends."

"Mrs. Sperling!" I groaned.

"Those were your tentative plans, weren't they?"

"Yes. Another educated guess?"

"Confirmed by your clothing." She ducked her head mischievously. "I'm sorry. That stumble was no accident. I was trying to confirm my guess. Spaghetti straps under your sweater and a full jersey skirt?"

"I wanted to look like a chauffeur and save time by not changing. You take as long as you want. My friends know I may not show."

"I don't want to take very long anyway. At this point, I'll use any excuse."

"Okay. You know your way up the drive?"

"Yes, thank you. Park the car around back, and don't worry about whistling loudly. I've pretty sharp ears."

"I can imagine."

I parked where she indicated, next to one of several limos already gathered. Another chauffeur headed into the back of the house, so I followed him. There were about eight of us in the brightly lit kitchen dodging the caterers. I was the only female in the group. I guess the guys figured I was with the caterers because they left me to myself at first. Then one noticed that I wasn't carrying trays and ambled over.

He was about my height, attractive, with dark

hair and a roundish face aged slightly with a thick mustache. He wore a black vest over a white shirt with a black tie and black pants.

"Hi. You're new," he said with an obvious sort of grin.

I smiled politely anyway.

"I'm Steve Lansky," he continued. "I drive for Ramona Bistler."

"You do?" My interest picked up a lot. "No kidding."

"No kidding. The boss told me I didn't have to wait. She'll probably be going home with some stud. I just stopped in to say hi to the guys. Looks like this is my lucky night."

"Maybe." I hesitated. On one hand, I wanted to keep his interest and possibly find something out about Ramona Bistler. On the other hand...

"Do you have to wait?" Lansky asked with a leer.

"Well, I... I might be able to get out of it. How do I get to the party?"

"Follow the trays, sweetheart. Tell you what, we'll go dancing, then..." He smirked. "We'll see what comes up."

"I'll go check."

I hurried after a tray laden young woman down a hall to a packed living room. Standing in the doorway, I began the first movement of Symphony Number Forty. It took a minute, but Mrs. Sperling appeared at my side.

"You're working very fast," she said softly.

"So's Bistler's chauffeur. He wants me to go

dancing with him."

"Convenient."

"It was his idea, I promise."

"I'm sure it was. It sounds like a golden opportunity."

"For information, yes."

"Not to your liking?"

"He thinks he's hot stuff."

"Don't sacrifice yourself, dear."

"It's no big deal. I put up with the jerk for an hour or so. I'll ditch him fast enough. In the meantime, I'll pump him for what he knows."

"It's not part of your job description."

"Maybe not, but I want to know."

"Good for you. Please wait here a minute."

She listened for a moment, then walked off across the room. I wondered where Eleanor was. The crowd shifted and I saw her tail listlessly thumping the floor from behind a sofa. Mrs. Sperling talked with Mrs. Delgado who nodded vigorously. Mrs. Sperling then threaded her way through the people back to me.

"The Delgados will give me a ride home," she said. "Go to your interrogation with my blessing and ditch the clod the moment you get a chance. I don't want you endangering yourself."

"I won't. Thanks."

"Oh, Delilah!" oozed an older woman as she slid up. Her skin was tan and freshly lifted, with perfect make-up and hair. "Darling, how did you get over here?"

"I walked," Mrs. Sperling answered with

irritated politeness.

"But how?"

"I stood and put one foot in front of the other. The same way you do."

"But there are so many people here. It must have been positively terrifying."

"Not in the least."

"Here, darling, let me help you back to the couch."

"I'd really rather mingle, thank you." Mrs. Sperling moved off into the swarm. If she bumped into anybody it was because the room was so crowded everyone was bumping into everyone else.

Taking a deep breath, I returned to my waiting swain. It took a little doing, but I convinced him that I really had to return the Mercedes to Mrs. Sperling's house. I also insisted on driving.

"I know a really hot spot in Westwood," I said when we were finally on our way in my Altima.

"Great."

"So how come your boss doesn't care where you leave her car?"

"Cause she's not going home in it. She doesn't care about nothing but getting laid and getting a good settlement from her husband. Or she cared about the settlement. Looks like she's getting the whole pile now."

"Yeah. She sure is lucky."

"She'd better watch her step. His family is supposed to contest the will. It's like before she had to be careful so no one caught her sleeping around so she could get plenty of alimony. If she wants that money, she's going to have to convince some judge she's a grieving, faithful widow."

"I hear she's not."

"You think your boss is weird. Mine is completely bananas. She's taken up joy riding lately. In fact, night before last she took off again. I know cause the gas tank was full the next morning."

"Full?"

"Yeah. She's trying to cover it up now. The tank was half empty when I left it that day. The next morning it's full. You try to tell me she didn't run it down driving all over kingdom come, then filled it up so I wouldn't think she'd been out."

"Did you hear the car running at all?"

"Nah. I was out all night. I tell you, the broad is crazy. Why should I care if she goes driving?"

"Beats me," I replied. He wouldn't care, all right. But she might, if she needed an alibi, and a car running in a garage does empty the tank.

I parked in a parking structure about a block from the disco, after getting Lansky to cough up the parking fee. It was a rotten move, considering what I'd just gotten, and what my intentions were. But Lansky got on my nerves.

I walked quickly to the disco. Lansky kept up but was a little winded when we reached the door. I got my hand stamped and went in with Lansky right there.

The music was good and loud and drowned him out. The generous dance floor was across from the bar, and busy but not overcrowded. Tables were scattered about and mostly filled. Single men and women stood about watching and plotting. I had to complete a circuit of the room to find my friends.

There were five of them, including a couple I didn't know very well. Their names were Jan and Lee. Tina Paulson, my best friend, stood when she saw me. Tina's a Black woman with a real exotic look that reminds me of Sade, only Tina's prettier. With her was her fiancé, Earl Cartwell, and a mutual friend, Mickey Dooley. Mickey has bright red hair and an outrageous personality. Besides dancing, Mickey is trying to break in as a stand-up comic. Tina's a dancer, like me, and Earl is a doctor. He was a second-year resident at U.C.L.A. Earl looks like a basketball player with a tall-skinny figure, dark chocolate skin, and close-cropped hair.

I said hello all around as best I could and didn't introduce Lansky. The set up was perfect. Mickey and I are old buddies. Mickey threw his arm around me and flagged down the cocktail waitress.

"Bring my lady here a gin and tonic," he yelled.

"Mickey, I'm driving!" I yelled back.

"So have some potato skins first. Here!" Mickey crammed a sour cream filled skin into my mouth. I laughed and tried not to get it all over my skirt. Out of the corner of my eye, I noticed Lansky sulkily pull up a chair and sit down. The next thing I knew, Mickey had pulled me onto the floor, and we were off.

I met Mickey in a partnering class in college. We danced together the second day and it was like we'd always been partners. Something just clicks when Mickey and I dance together. It took a year of dating to find out our partnership was limited to the dance floor. But we're still good friends, and we love to go dancing.

I hoped that when Lansky saw me and Mickey he'd throw in the towel. No such luck. I have to give the guy some credit for persistence. He even managed to get something of a conversation going with Earl.

Unfortunately, I had to share Mickey. Earl dances, but he's such a klutz Tina goes crazy if she doesn't get to dance with Mickey every so often. I decided to rest.

"So why don't we blow this joint?" Lansky said in my ear.

I noticed he was drinking from my gin and tonic.

"Why?" I asked. "I'm having a blast."

"What about something coming up?"

"The only thing coming up around here is the dance contest, and Mickey and I are going to win it."

"But you came here with me."

"Lansky, face it. This relationship is going nowhere. You're an okay guy, but you're not my type. It was a nice try. I appreciate it."

Lansky grumbled something and left. Tina came up and dared me to go to the bathroom with her. Laughing, I went.

Tina wanted to know who Lansky was, so I told her as she washed her hands. That led to Mrs. Sperling's generous arrangement with my career.

"You lucked out," said Tina. She turned off the water.

"You're telling me."

"But this murder thing. Is she a cop?"

"Well, a private eye."

Tina looked around for a towel. "No shit."

"By all accounts, she's pretty good at it."

"Sounds kind of creepy to me."

"Hey, the bucks are coming in, and I'm not living at home. I couldn't ask for more."

"Yes, you could." She shook droplets of water all over me. "How about a leading role in a major motion picture starring also your best friend?"

"And how about an Oscar on top of that?"

"How about several million dollars?"

"How about numberless gorgeous men falling at my feet?"

"How about... Oh, damn! You topped me again."

I pushed her out of the restroom.

Mickey and I won the dance contest, but I have to admit it was close. I knew the other couple were pros also. I'd seen them at auditions. I offered Mickey the prize money since I was working.

"No, my dear," he replied. "We'll split as usual. I just signed a contract with a lovely little club down in Hollywood. It's called the Laugh Factory."

"Mickey! That's wonderful!" I screamed and

threw my arms around him.

"It seems you've heard of it. I'll only be there for three weeks. But the pay should feed me for somewhat longer. I've got some residuals, too, so I'm in the black for the time being."

We all danced a while longer then mutually decided to call it a night. Earl and Tina left first with Jan and Lee. Mickey and I did one more song, then Mickey insisted on walking me back to my car.

It was the element of surprise that knocked Mickey over. Neither of us could figure out quite what happened. We were almost to my car on the top floor of the parking structure when suddenly Mickey landed on his backside and my head was in a hammerlock. Lansky's voice slurred as he cursed me.

"What's Sperling got on me?" he growled. "Huh? What's she got?"

He choked me so badly I couldn't speak. Then I fell under two bodies, each scrambling for the other. Groaning, I managed to crawl out from under Lansky and Mickey.

They rolled together. Mickey showed on top and pulled back for a punch. It landed on Lansky's jaw but didn't do much. Lansky latched onto Mickey's throat. Mickey broke the hold but fell backward. Lansky popped up. Mickey dodged just in time and staggered to his feet. So did Lansky.

The two men gasped as they glared at each other. Lansky danced in and swung first. It connected with Mickey's eye. He faded back as

Lansky came in again, this time to the stomach. Mickey got in a punch to Lansky's nose. Lansky landed two more in Mickey's stomach. Mickey stepped back and bumped into the retaining wall. Lansky grinned. His hands shot out and grabbed Mickey by the throat. Mickey grabbed on for dear life.

I watched in horror. At first, I couldn't even yell, I was so scared. Lansky started pushing Mickey over the wall. That's when I got angry. I ran over and pounded on Lansky's back. Mickey broke his grasp and pounded on Lansky's front. Lansky sagged to the ground.

"Oh no." I started crying. "Is he still alive?"

Mickey checked him. "Oh, yeah. He'll be sore in the morning but fine."

"Are you okay?"

We staggered over to my car.

"I'm fine." Mickey slid on his best Irish brogue. "I'm an Irishman. I love a good fight."

"Mickey, that's not funny. And you're half Swedish. Are you sure you're okay?"

"Yes, I'm fine." He held me by my shoulders and looked into my eyes. "I relaxed with the punches, and he didn't hurt me."

"Okay."

I sniffed again and Mickey kissed me. It was one of those wonderful, full kisses that had kept us dating for a year. We both sighed as we came apart.

"It's mighty tempting," Mickey said. "We wouldn't last five minutes, but it's mighty tempting."

"You think...? No. No way. I don't want to get messed up in that again. What are we going to do about him?"

"Leave him. You gonna come see me at the Laugh Factory?"

"With as many friends as I can drag down there."

"Great. I'll call you."

"Or I'll call you. As soon as the next dance contest comes up."

"Right." He took my keys and opened my car door for me. "There you are, my lady."

"Thank you, my lord."

He shut the door for me, then waited while I coaxed the Altima's engine into starting. We waved as I drove off.

Glen's door was open when I got home, leading me to deduce that he was still out. A frigid breeze blew into the hallway from his open window. I didn't know if Mrs. Sperling was up or not. No lights were on, but that didn't mean anything. I knew she was home. She'd left a note on the bulletin board between Glen's and my rooms informing us that there was no need to be up early as she had no plans and was absolutely not going to receive.

I took advantage of it and slept until noon. I beat Glen to the bathroom. He was still in there when the phone rang. It was my mother wanting to know if I was coming to Sunday dinner the next day. I told her I'd call her back after I'd talked to Mrs. Sperling.

I decided to try the kitchen first. At bare minimum, I'd get something to eat. Mrs. Osgood was there, putting together a tray.

"Mrs. Sperling is not feeling well today," she explained. "Will you bring this up for her?"

"Sure. Can I eat first?"

"You should."

"I'll get it. I thought I saw some cereal in the

cupboard."

I had. Glen came in as I got out the milk.

"She's having one of her days," he grumbled.

"Mrs. Sperling?" I asked.

"Yes." Glen morosely removed a bowl from the cabinet. "She has two kinds. A kind where she just doesn't feel like getting out of bed. Those are okay. Then she has sick days. Those are totally awful. I gotta be around to carry trays, but she doesn't get many, so I'm stuck waiting all day."

"You could do homework," volunteered Mrs. Osgood.

"I should, but it's totally boring."

"You're in school?" I asked.

"Yeah. U.C.L.A."

"No kidding. My best friend's fiancé is a resident at the medical center there. What's your major?"

"Psych."

"The tray is ready," Mrs. Osgood broke in.

"I'll take it up," I said. "I've got to talk to Mrs. Sperling anyway. I haven't got anything better to do, so if you want to ditch, Glen, why don't you?"

He grinned. "You don't mind? Awesome."

I put my bowl in the sink and picked up the tray. Mrs. Sperling's room was dark. Light filtered through the sheer curtains on the long window leaving a square patch on the king-sized bed. Eleanor lay curled up at the bed's foot. She looked as dismal as her mistress.

Mrs. Sperling was on her back in the middle of the bed with an ice pack covering her eyes.

"Mm?" she softly moaned as I entered.

"It's me, Donna. Mrs. Osgood sent me up with this tray."

"Put it on the bedside table."

"There's tea here and some toast." I set the tray down where she'd asked. "You wouldn't happen to be suffering from a migraine, would you?"

She winced. "You would have to guess that. I hate admitting it, but I am. I'm not the fuzzy slipper type."

"Actually, highly creative and intelligent women are more likely to get them."

"Where did you read that?"

"I was told by my doctor when I had one. It's not an experience I'd like to repeat."

"I wouldn't wish it on Alisa Montrose, even though she is probably behind this one." She winced.

"Was she the lady last night who was so surprised that you could get from one end of a room to the other without killing yourself?"

"Yes."

"May her face fall even faster this time. I felt like punching her."

"I abhor violence. If it wouldn't be so unfair to the poor person, I'd wish arthritis on her plastic surgeon." She sighed loudly. "It's so aggravating, Donna. Why can't people understand I can get along, in many ways, just as well as they can?"

"I don't know. It seems amazing to me that you do, especially when I think of how much I use my sight. We used to do trust walks in my acting classes. We closed our eyes and just walked, trusting that our classmates would catch us before we bumped into anything. It was the scariest feeling. And yet you do it all the time. It's hard for me to understand how."

"It must be as hard for you to imagine being blind as it is for me to imagine seeing. There's no sense in it, though. Why do some people insist on treating me like glass when the evidence of my capabilities is thrown in their faces?"

"They're blind to it?"

That got a chuckle out of her. "Certainly in the case of Alisa Montrose. My heavens, that woman is disgusting. She yells at me as if I were deaf, holds me up as if I were a cripple, then gushes on incessantly about what a miracle I've achieved in spite of my tragic affliction. I ask you, is there anything tragic about me?"

"Well, you're a widow."

"That isn't tragic. Heartbreaking, but not tragic. If anything, John's death was rather mundane."

"It was?"

"Yes. He had your basic heart attack. It all happened almost ten years ago, and he died almost instantly. He understood, and he was a cinematographer, one of the best. His eyes were his living, and yet he rarely noticed my lack of sight."

"You still miss him."

"A husband is a hard thing to lose. Still, I'm a strong person. There is a great deal of truth in time's healing powers. Sometimes I think that's Alisa's whole problem. I've had it fairly easy, but that woman has never known a moment's adversity. The worse trauma she's suffered is a broken fingernail. Poor thing, she deserves pity. Of the two of us, I'd say she's the handicapped one. A lack of basic intelligence is far more devastating, don't you think?"

"To those who have to put up with her, it is. She probably doesn't know the difference."

"She doesn't." Mrs. Sperling suddenly smiled. "It's terrible how that woman brings out my worse instincts. I was unforgivably rude to her last night, and worse yet, I thoroughly enjoyed it."

"What happened?"

"She was displaying her Niedeman serigraph, the HN4. She was bragging about it, when I, with tremendous pleasure, informed her that it was a fake. She was aghast. How could I possibly know? I couldn't see it. I pointed out that she could, and it hadn't stopped her from being fooled. Of course, she wouldn't believe me, so I told her about the smell, just to prove I knew what I was talking about. I doubt she believed me even after that, but Norma Delgado said she heard Alisa mention something about an appraisal later."

"Was it a fake?"

"Certainly. Do you think I would risk her calling my bluff? Furthermore, she got it from Mr. Stein."

"So maybe he is counterfeiting."

"Possibly. I also ran into the son of some old

friends of my family. Phillip has been collecting Niedemans since before the artist's death. He, naturally, has all the commemoratives. I overheard his comment that he was very unlikely to end up in Alisa's predicament, even though he'd recently made a purchase. I found it interesting that he was so certain of his serigraph's authenticity. So later I managed to obtain an invitation to look at his sculptures on Monday afternoon."

"Okay. Is there anything planned for tomorrow?"

"You may have the day off after church. Do you belong to any?"

"Not really."

"Fine. You will accompany me then. I am a practicing Catholic, and I hold the Church's view that a little religion once a week is essential for personal growth, even if that is a minimum. Unless you have some serious objections."

"No. I guess not. I'm Catholic, too, but I haven't been to church in a while."

"A providential meeting, then. We'll be going to nine o'clock mass, after that you'll be free."

"Fine. My mom wants me to go home for dinner. My brother and his fiancée are coming."

"That should be pleasant. Did you find anything out from Mr. Lansky?"

"Oh boy, did I." I told her the whole story. She tsk'd over the fight.

"I shouldn't have let you go. I was afraid there might be trouble. Was Mr. Lansky hurt?"

"Mickey didn't think so. Lansky was pretty

looped, too."

"It's fortunate that your friend was there, although I deplore the necessity."

I shrugged. "Mickey probably enjoyed it. That's one of the reasons we never made it as a couple. I can't handle fighting, and Mickey loves it. He was always trying to get some debate going with me. I hated it, and he hated it when I refused to argue back."

"All for the better then. Mr. Lansky wanted to know what I had on him?"

"Yeah. I never told him who I worked for. I figured he overheard me talking about you to my friends and realized I was pumping him and got scared. But why?"

"That is the question. Another piece for the puzzle and precious few of them are fitting with any other."

"Did you get to talk with Ramona Bistler?"

"Only long enough to secure an invitation to her home sometime this week. What you've just told me shall make it an interesting visit indeed." She paused. "You say this Mickey is just a friend of yours."

"Alright," I groaned. "He is now. We tried, but just didn't work, and it never will."

"Indeed, and all the more painful because you two truly care for each other." She yawned.

"I guess I ought to take off. Feeling any better?"

"Some. I expect I shall have to just sleep it off. Would you please take Eleanor on a walk for me?"

"Sure. Eleanor, come."

Eleanor got up slowly, looked back at her mistress, then padded out of the room at my side.

My whole family showed up on Sunday. It made for quite a crowd around the table, especially since my brother's fiancée, Elise, and my brother-in-law, Ernie, were there also. My other sister, Denise, and I were the only singles left, something Peter made a point of rubbing in. He also made a couple cracks about the odds against Debbie's marriage working out. Ernie just laughed and said he was used to beating the odds. Debbie laughed also, but I could tell she wanted to slug Peter one. Elise did.

"Hey!" Peter yelped.

"You quit being so snotty," reprimanded Elise.

"That's right, Elise," I cheered. "Keep him in line."

"Thanks, Donna." Peter glared at me.

"Children," sighed my father.

"Let's not get into an argument," Mom cut in.

"So, how's the drug-making business?" Debbie asked.

Peter's a chemist for a pharmaceutical company in Pasadena.

"Good," replied Peter, ignoring Debbie's cut. None of us would ever let Peter live down that he was into drugs for a living. "I'm working." He looked right at me.

"So am I," I said with a slight grin.

"I heard. Driving a car. Some great career that is."

"I think it's a perfectly good one," said Denise.

"It's honest work, for one thing."

"And I can still work on my acting career," I added.

"Still thinking about that, huh?" Dad asked with a worried frown.

Mom sighed. "I hope you're not endangering your job."

"Not in the least." I squirmed under Peter's grin. "Mrs. Sperling says it's perfectly alright. In fact, she's encouraging it."

"That is terrific," said Denise. "I wish I had a boss like that."

"It sure is nice of her, isn't it, Peter?" Elise looked at him. Peter didn't answer.

"Mom says you're living in Beverly Hills," said Debbie, still trying to get Peter back.

"Yeah. It's a real nice house. I've got my own room, but I do have to share a bathroom with the houseboy. He is a slob, too. He's into collecting Niedemans."

"Really? I just got one this morning, the HN4," said Peter.

"No kidding. Where?" I asked.

"A little place down in Hollywood. This lady owns it. She always sells them cheap."

"You got it this morning? That's weird."

"I know. I got a hell of a deal. I get all my Niedemans there. I'm on the broad's waiting list. I've been looking for HN4 for a while. Then yesterday she called me and said she'd found a couple extra and did I still want one. I hot-footed it out there this morning and grabbed it."

"Peter is such a sexist," sighed Elise. "Have you seen those prints?"

"Just the one," I said. "And you're right."

"I've seen a whole bunch," said Debbie. "Peter, your taste is despicable."

"That's not fair," Denise said. "Niedeman's women are idealized, the embodiment of the perfect woman. I think they're fascinating." Denise is an art major.

Peter laughed. "I'm just buying them for the investment value, and, Elise, you know it. The guy is still hot, and the prices are going up."

"Only because he's dead," said Debbie.

Denise shook her head. "Not necessarily. He was very popular before he died."

"Either way," I snickered. "Peter, are you sure you haven't got a counterfeit?"

"Yeah, I'm sure," Peter retorted.

"I might be able to tell," said Denise.

"So can I," I said, smugly.

"Since when are you such an expert?" said Peter.

"Since Glen Weir got stuck with a fake."

"Who's he?"

"Mrs. Sperling's houseboy. She spotted it and told me how."

"Well, most knock-offs of Niedemans are easy to tell because they're such bad quality," Denise said.

"These are really good ones, Denise." I smiled. "Most people can't see the difference."

"Well, my supplier could," bragged Peter. "She

may be pretty flakey, but she knows her art."

"Flakey?" I asked. "How?"

Peter shrugged. "She's old, and she dresses like she's from the sixties, and she's a space cadet, keeps talking about her past lives."

"Dolores Carmine!" I almost jumped.

"You know her?" Peter was as shocked as I was.

"I've met her. Mrs. Sperling knows her. We were checking out Glen's fake."

I must admit I enjoyed the sick look that came over Peter's face just then. As soon as we finished eating, he had Denise look over his print. She said it looked good. I sniffed it but couldn't be sure.

At about two thirty Peter couldn't take it anymore and talked me into following him to Hollywood in my car and going to see Dolores Carmine. It wasn't too hard. I wanted to talk to Dolores, also. Fake or real, the source of that print could be important. I could just see Mrs. Sperling's gratified smile.

Most of the stores on Dolores' block were closed. But there was a light on in the gallery. I held Peter and Elise back.

"Peter, I've got some very specific questions to ask," I said. "So will you please let me do the talking, and play along?"

"Why?" he asked.

"Just trust me."

"Peter, can you please?" Elise asked.

"Alright."

I led the way in. Nothing had changed in the

musty old shop. Dolores shuffled in from the back, muttering obscenities. She smiled when she saw me.

"Hello, little bitch," she said, grinning, then noticed Peter and Elise. "And you two shits are back."

"They're with me," I said. "Mrs. Sperling wanted them to come. She asked me to ask you a few questions about the serigraph you sold them this morning. She's kind of tied up right now, or she would've come herself."

Dolores shrugged noncommittally. "What the fuck."

"Where did you get it? Peter, here, told me you'd just got some others in."

"Yeah. This young prick came by and sold them to me cheap."

"What was his name?"

"Do I fucking look like I'd ask?"

"Do you remember what he looked like?"

"Tallish with dishwater hair."

"Are the prints genuine?"

"Fuck, yes."

"But how do you know if you don't know the person who sold them to you?"

"He said he was a friend of Fred Gonzagos."

"Those aren't exactly the best credentials."

"Fred's not gonna stick me with shit. He knows better, and he's a friend anyway."

"Speaking of Fred, have you talked to him lately?"

"Not since early last week."

"Any idea where he is?"

Dolores frowned. "Why? Is he missing?"

"Yep. Since Wednesday night. If you hear anything, will you let Mrs. Sperling know?"

"I suppose." She stopped and looked at me. "I knew you. You were a queen, a Goth queen. Do you remember?"

"Uh, no."

"I was a Roman decurion. You bore three sons for me."

"Great. Listen, Mrs. Sperling's waiting for me. I've gotta run. Thanks for the answers."

I pushed Peter and Elise out of the shop ahead of me.

"She said I saved her from an evil wizard," Peter chuckled.

"I never knew you were that noble," I returned.

"He has his moments," said Elise.

I remembered there was something she saw in him. My sisters and I could never quite figure out what. Peter can be charming and warm, but all my sisters and I usually saw was his more odious side. I have to be fair. We weren't always very pleasant to him.

"Listen," I said. "I don't want to take Dolores's word on that print."

"Why not?" asked Peter.

"Because Fred Gonzagos happens to be a counterfeiter of fine artwork."

"You know some pretty interesting people," teased Elise.

"I don't know him." I sighed. I didn't dare take

a chance on letting it get back to my mom that I was mixed up in a murder. "Mrs. Sperling thinks that Glen's fake was done by this Gonzagos guy. It's a long story. Anyway, why don't I take your print and have Mrs. Sperling check it out? I'll get it back to you Monday, Tuesday at the latest, I promise."

Peter grumbled. "Oh, alright. You got my work phone?"

"Sure. Or will Elise be at your apartment?"

"Of course," Elise replied. "I don't go into the store until five Monday and Tuesday."

"Elise." Peter shifted with the guilty warning.

I laughed. "Don't tell me..."

"Yeah, she's already there," sighed Peter.

"Don't tell our parents, please?" Elise begged. "My old roommate's covering for me. My dad'd kill me if he knew."

"Oh, I wouldn't tell the folks," I said. "But I'd sure like to tell Debbie."

"Donna!" Peter groaned. "Come on. We're already getting married."

"Okay. But no more cracks about her and Ernie."

Peter nodded reluctantly and went and got the print. It was rolled up in a large cardboard tube. I put it in my car and again talked the motor into running.

I got my gratified smile Sunday evening. Mrs. Sperling didn't say whether or not my information meant anything. I got the feeling it fit in with some hypothesis she had, and she was holding her cards close to her chest, so to speak.

The next morning, I got back from dance class and cleaned up just barely in time to drive Mrs. Sperling to the Braille Institute, on Vermont. I thumbed through my Backstage Magazine while she tutored Delsie Simmons, a young black girl recently blinded in an altercation. One of the aides told me that Mrs. Sperling always got the tough ones because she was the only one who could handle them.

Delsie was not only prone to skipping her homework, she was also very belligerent, and had yet to accept her handicap. I got a little nervous when I heard yelling coming from the room. It soon stopped and eventually, Mrs. Sperling came out unscathed and unruffled. She waited until Delsie had left the building before giving me our next destination.

It was a luxury condo nestled in one of those high rises along Wilshire, just past the crossing with Santa Monica Boulevard. I don't know if that's Beverly Hills proper, or West Los Angeles, but it's still rich kid country, and not far from U.C.L.A. Being help, I got to park the car myself after Mrs. Sperling had been helped out of the car by the building's doorman. She was waiting in the lobby for me when I got back.

"What took so long?" she asked.

"They don't have visitor parking here," I grumbled. "Parking in this city is insane."

Mrs. Sperling nodded. "I understand it's worse in New York."

"That's what I hear. Know where the elevator is?"

"Actually, no. Why don't I just take your elbow?"

I looked around, searching for the conveyance, then took off at a brisk pace. Mrs. Sperling matched it, with Eleanor matching us both.

"He said it was three doors down to the right," Mrs. Sperling said as we got off on the twelfth floor.

She and Eleanor took the lead from there. The door opened seconds after Mrs. Sperling rang and he ushered us in. I saw the condo first. It was mostly a huge living room furnished in black, white, and royal blue minimalist with a long window taking up most of one wall and which overlooked Wilshire Boulevard and the condominiums across the street. The view made me woozy. I looked away. In the center of the room, a spiral staircase led to a loft. Under the loft was a tiny kitchen which matched the living room, and a black and glass dining room.

Then I saw Him. Tall and slender, with a chest that was just broad enough, lightly tanned skin, a fabulous face and beautiful, laughing green eyes. His sun bleached hair was dark rooted and clipped and arranged with stylish abandon. I'd seen His dark bomber jacket, yellow print shirt and baggy pants on mannequins on Rodeo Drive. Not that exact ensemble, but things like it.

It was Phillip DuPre, live and incredibly handsome, right in front of me. I was in shock. I mean, I figured Mrs. Sperling might have a few industry contacts, having been married to a cinematographer and all. But Hollywood's latest golden boy director? A guy who had directed two mega-hit feature films, among other things, and now had every big name in music screaming at Him to do their videos? This was the son of some old family friends?

I had first seen Him at a cattle call for His second rock video. The first was from His movie "Five Alarm", and that was the one that got the music industry so excited. He was behind the table with the casting director and producer, although He was obviously in charge. I remember joking with Tina that I would have loved a chance to fall in love with Him.

At the time, of course, it was ridiculous. I was just one of a thousand dancers who were auditioning for a role. He'd smiled at me. He'd smiled at all of us. I got called back, and He smiled at me again. I didn't get the role. I don't know if it was intense jealousy that she was working with that gorgeous man and I wasn't, but I did not like the girl they chose.

"Phillip, I'd like you to meet my new chauffeur, Donna Brechter," Mrs. Sperling was saying.

It dawned on me I'd been so busy ogling I hadn't heard or seen any of the traditional greetings.

"Hi," He said, pleasantly. He held out His hand.

"Hi," I said.

Really winning dialogue, I know, but my heart was pounding so hard I couldn't think straight. The man was just that gorgeous. I remembered to shake His hand, only He'd already started withdrawing it. I grabbed, He fumbled. It went back and forth for an hour, it seemed like. Mrs. Sperling says I didn't, but I turned three shades of purple.

He laughed, quiet and really cute, then looked at me again.

"You've auditioned for me, haven't you?" He asked.

"You remember?" I was in seventh heaven.

He actually blushed. "Well, not quite. It's something more along Aunt Delilah's line. Uh, deductive reasoning. I'm pretty good at faces, and if I can't attach a place to one, I probably saw it at an audition. You look vaguely familiar, but nothing else, ergo..."

"Yeah. It was for the 'White Heat' video. I got called back."

"Right. I remember now." He smiled even more warmly if that were possible. "You were good."

"Thanks."

"Phillip, I believe you have some sculpture to show me?" broke in Mrs. Sperling.

"Yeah. It's right this way. Would you like me to take you around the room first?"

"Thank you, Phillip. That would be quite nice."

He took her elbow and guided her around the room, letting her place the furniture, warning her about a wobbly stand here, or a sharp corner there. His Niedemans hung all over, the only other colors in the room besides the main decor. They were all in thick black lacquered frames. He had several bronze sculptures and some clay ones, and one beautiful white porcelain figure of a woman. It was to these pieces that He drew Mrs. Sperling's attention.

"A Remington?" Mrs. Sperling chuckled, going over a bronze of a cowboy on a bronc.

"I have my moments." He shrugged. "Besides, that's investment art. I got a good deal on it and give me a few years and I'll get a hell of a profit on it. In fact, I've got a signed Ansel Adams print in the dining room. I could get some real bucks on that."

"Your deals are legendary, Phillip," replied Mrs. Sperling. Everything He did was legendary. But Mrs. Sperling seemed immune to it. She moved to another bronze. "And what have we here?"

"Now that was a real find." He leaned against

the back of the black leather sofa and folded His arms across His chest. "It's a bronze by Hans Niedeman. I got it about a year before he died. They're really rare. He did not do many of them. It's like the Remington, in that the sculpture is almost a three-dimensional version of the painting."

"So, this is what all the fuss is about."

"That and the investment value. Most of it isn't worth that much, more for rich teenagers and upper-middle-class types. But I've got some signed pieces that will bring in some money. I'm glad I got into it when I did. It saved me a few bucks."

Mrs. Sperling laughed. "Young man, when have you ever wanted for anything? You are as penurious as your father."

He shrugged. "Dad made sure I knew the value of a buck. You know the industry. I'm doing good now, but it won't necessarily last. I gotta invest in something to keep me comfortable when the glow fades."

"Phillip, I find your complete grasp of reality utterly refreshing." Mrs. Sperling smiled at Him with genuine affection. "And your lack of an over-inflated ego even more so."

"Who can keep an ego with two younger brothers? Say, Aunt Delilah, have you seen Richard lately?"

"He's not back from law school already, is he?"

"No. But I heard you were back east last week. I thought maybe you had."

"Briefly. Jimmy's tour kicked off, and I visited

a few friends, but I didn't leave New York."

"Richard's graduating this December, and at the top of his class. He is so thrilled. He wants you at the graduation."

"I wouldn't dream of missing it." Mrs. Sperling cleared her throat.

I remembered my job. I wandered over to the HN4 where it hung by the window, out of which I refused to look. Reminding myself that I was twelve stories above solid ground was not going to do my nerves any good.

"My brother just got one of these," I said.

"One of what?" Mrs. Sperling walked over to me.

"This Niedeman print. He says it's one of the commemoratives."

"Well, Aunt Delilah?" He ambled over. "Real or fake?"

She sniffed. "The smell seems genuine, so it's not one of the fakes I've been chasing. Where did you get it?"

He held up his hands. "Sorry. Gotta protect my sources."

"Phillip. I'm certainly the last person to be creating competition."

"Aunt Delilah, I'd love to tell you. But the guy is real nervous. He's getting me some terrific deals, and I don't want to ruin it on an accidental slip of the tongue. Besides, I promised I wouldn't."

"I see." She didn't believe Him for some reason.

"I bet you do. How about if I offer lunch as a consolation prize, including your dancer hyphen chauffeur."

"That sounds worthwhile."

Mrs. Sperling didn't press the issue.

He insisted on driving us in His BMW. Mrs. Sperling insisted on sitting in the back with Eleanor, which meant I had to sit up front. I was heartbroken. I tried to make some intelligent small talk, but what do you say to a god?

Mrs. Sperling kept the conversational ball rolling and even set up a few opportunities for my brilliant wit and dazzling charm to shine out. I managed not to get tongue-tied and sounded like I had a reasonable command of the language. Other than that, I was pretty quiet.

He was kind of quiet, too, which surprised me a little. At the audition, He'd seemed really outgoing, the kind of person who knows He's in charge but doesn't have to ram it down everyone's throat. He answered Mrs. Sperling's questions about His family and other little things. He smiled at me. I smiled back, trying not to melt.

We ended up at this little eatery in Santa Monica where several more distinguished members of the Industry were dining. After having been dazzled by Phillip DuPre, and I confess, still under His spell, these other big shots had no impact on me whatsoever. I was so cool, it was disgusting.

It was very satisfying, too, when our waitress just happened to be this little witch I knew from my dance class who was a horrible name dropper and treated me like I was the biggest no-talent in

Southern California. She recognized Phillip DuPre immediately. And there I was, having lunch with Him, and on a first name basis. It was certainly one of my better days.

Mrs. Sperling waited until we were eating dessert before bringing up the murder.

"Phillip," she began, after wrapping her hands around a cup of very good cappuccino. "I know you think you have very good reasons for keeping your friend's name from me, but please consider, your supplier could know something related to Joshua Stein's death."

He winced. "Uh, yeah. I suppose it could."

Mrs. Sperling sighed. "You know very well it could, young man. I don't want you doing anything foolish."

"I'm not going—"

"Phillip."

He grimaced. "Tell you what. I'll talk to my source. If he agrees, I'll set up a meeting between you two. Will that redeem me?"

Mrs. Sperling smiled with maternal affection. "It's a start."

After lunch, we went back and got the Lexus. We paid a call on Sergeant Michaelson, who growled that there were no new developments. We tried to pay a call on Ramona Bistler, but she was gone. In desperation, Mrs. Sperling directed me to Dolores Carmine's. She was in, but not much help.

"You have no idea where Fred Gonzagos might be?" Mrs. Sperling pressed.

"If I had, I would've told you," replied Dolores.

"What did he say the last time you saw him?"

"Nothing. He complained about the capitalist fucks and how they don't recognize his art, and I sympathized. He asked me to loan him a few bucks. I said go piss up a rope. I don't have a few bucks."

"What did he want the money for?"

"For a few drinks. What else? The way that son of a bitch drinks, it would take more than a few bucks to get him drunk. But, shit. That's his problem. I can barely eat as it is."

"Did he say anything about going anywhere?"

"Just to his favorite bar. Hennessy's. Down on Sunset, near La Cienega. It's an okay place. A little too capitalist for my tastes. But it's okay."

"About this latest shipment of Niedemans, how many did you get?"

"Shit, about five of them."

"That's a lot."

Dolores just shrugged. "Since when am I gonna argue with some asshole who wants wholesale cost for them? I grabbed the whole bunch."

"Did it occur to you they might be hot?"

"Why would I think something like that? Fuck, yes, I thought they might be. But I didn't ask questions. I'm not stupid. Besides, he was Fred's friend. Fred don't send me no shit."

"And Fred is missing. Does he have any relatives that you know of?"

"A sister, I think. Maybe an ex-wife. I don't know any names."

"Somehow, I'm not surprised. Well, thank you, Dolores. You've been exceptionally kind."

"Right. See you later."

We went back to Beverly Hills to find out what company was the private security patrol around Mr. Stein's gallery. We did get that name. We drove out to their offices only to find that the guard who had been patrolling the night of the murder was sick, and, no, the receptionist could not give out his address or phone number.

Before giving up, Mrs. Sperling had me take her to the Beverly Hills P.D. again. There, she tried to get the girl in the records department to see if Fred Gonzagos had a file in the national crime computer. The girl said she couldn't. Mrs. Sperling had her call the chief. The chief had already gone home for the day.

"That settles it," said Mrs. Sperling. "It's a sign from God. We may as well go home. Eleanor, forward."

In the car, I tried to cheer her up.

"We'll get the record tomorrow," I said. "I'll run over there first thing after dance class. Or I could even skip dance class."

"Oh no. Don't do that."

"I don't mind."

"Darling, you need to keep in shape. I also agreed to support your efforts."

"You don't have to. I mean, I'm working for you. You get first priority."

"Which I'll take when I need it."

"I have an idea. I'll call a couple of my friends

and we'll go out to that Hennessey's bar tonight. I'll ask around for Fred and see what I find. If he's truly a regular, someone will know him."

"Donna, you do realize that could be dangerous."

"I'll call Mickey. He loves a good fight, remember?"

"I do. I hope that is the least of the trouble you find." Mrs. Sperling sighed. "There is a possibility that Mr. Gonzagos is a pre-meditated killer, and he may not appreciate someone trying to find him. It's also not unlikely that someone else again might not want Mr. Gonzagos found."

"I'll lie about my identity. No big."

"It could be. You're as bad as Phillip. The both of you have this fantasy of playing detective. This isn't a child's game of cops and robbers. We're looking for a cold-blooded murderer."

"I know basic self-defense. And I don't see you carrying a gun."

"That doesn't mean I don't."

"But—"

"If I can hear it, I can hit it, and my hearing is very good. I've been fortunate that I've hardly had to use it. I might also add that there's a gun in the glove compartment of each of my cars. Just keep in mind the objective is not to use it."

"You really think I might need a gun if I go to Hennessy's tonight?"

"Probably not. But it could stir up trouble."

"Yick. On the other hand, it could probably help things."

"True." There was a pause. "Very well. Call your friends if you wish. However, before you go, we will go over the proper use of firearms, and you will carry one. You're not permitted for it, but I'd rather pay a fine than for a funeral."

"So reassuring. You sure you don't want to come along?"

"No. It's better that you go without me. I'm hardly inconspicuous."

Dinner was ready when we got back to the house. I called Tina and Mickey right away, then sat down to eat. Earl was working that night, so Tina was looking for an excuse to get out. Mickey just wanted to go, and a bar suited him fine.

I didn't tell them I was packing a heater, as they say. I knew how to shoot it, too. Mrs. Sperling made sure of that and promised I'd get some time on a shooting range in the near future.

Hennessey's was a pretty basic place. A nice restaurant lurked beyond the bar, which was dark and decorated in a pseudo-Victorian style. In one corner a huge projection T.V. displayed a football game. A crowd had gathered around it and cheered on one of the teams. I think it was the Rams, Forty-Niners game, but that might have been the following week. I don't remember, which is odd because I'm an ardent Rams fan.

Mickey and Tina groaned when they saw me heading for the television. Mickey all but picked me up and sat me down at the bar.

"You've got other things to do," he told me.

Tina and I ordered white wine and Mickey got

a gin and tonic. The bartender returned with the drinks grumbling about the game. He was bent over and balding and looked as though he'd been mixing drinks since before he was legal.

"You here a lot?" I asked.

"Most every night."

"There's this guy, his name's Fred Gonzagos. I've heard he sells artwork. Somebody told me he likes to do his drinking here."

"Yeah, he does. Hasn't been in while though."

"When was the last time you saw him?"

"Last Wednesday." He squinted at me. "You a cop?"

"Me?" I started. "Are you kidding? I just want to track Fred down. I heard he's got Niedemans for sale, and he's the only person in town who's got 'em. I gotta get one."

"Well, if he had 'em, they're all sold by now. He came in here Wednesday pretty happy and with a bit more cash than usual. Said he sold some art. Must be them Niedemans you're talking about."

"What time was he here?"

"Early evening, I think. I remember it was later than normal. He missed happy hour. I do know that. He often comes in and eats the hors-d'oeuvres for dinner. Must have been closer to nine, now that I think about it. Bought a couple rounds for these two girls, then made some stupid joke about saving some money for gas."

I swallowed. "No kidding. You wouldn't happen to know if he has any relatives or friends that might know where he is, would you?"

"Well, he spends a lot of time cussing out his sister when he gets drunk. I believe her name is Anita. Think she's married, too."

"Oh. Great. Well, thanks for the info."

We only stayed long enough to finish our drinks. I wanted to watch the rest of the football game, but Tina insisted we go someplace either a little quieter or with dancing. We got stuck with the quieter. Most places don't have dancing on Monday nights. Mickey was disappointed that things had gone so smoothly.

The next morning, I visited the police station briefly after class. When I got home, I was surprised to see the kitchen empty. Voices floated in from the dining room.

"Has she considered a breast augmentation?" asked one, a male voice. My heart stopped. It was His.

"Phillip!" gasped Mrs. Sperling.

"It's a professional issue," He protested.

"Phillip."

"Aw, come on, Aunt Delilah. You know that doesn't turn me on. I think she's perfectly gorgeous the way she is. But it wouldn't hurt her career, and we both know it."

Mrs. Sperling coughed, then called, "Why don't you come in, Donna?"

They were having brunch, spinach souffle, and baked applesauce. Mrs. Sperling invited me to join them.

"I, uh, don't exactly smell good," I protested. "I've been working out."

"Won't bother me any," He said, staring at His plate for some reason.

"It's well within bearable limits for me," added Mrs. Sperling. "And you need to eat."

"Well, uh, thanks." I sat down nervously and helped myself.

"Donna, what was your agent's name?" asked Mrs. Sperling.

"The theatrical one I'm giving up?"

"You are?" He finally looked at me.

I felt myself blush and really worked at sounding cool and calm. "I'm not getting sent out on enough auditions. It has been a slow season but not that slow. My friend, Tina, has gone out on three or four and got called back twice."

"Is your friend, Tina, a dancer?" He asked.

"Yeah. She's really good, and beautiful. She has this really exotic look, almost like a cross between a Black and an Asian, only she's all Black. She's real pretty and a terrific actress."

"We want to know your agent's name, dear," pressed Mrs. Sperling.

"Jerry Lawton, over at Lawton, Wheaton, and Weiss," I said.

"Sh—" He saw Mrs. Sperling's frown and shook His head. "Him."

"You seem to know him," said Mrs. Sperling.

"The man is scum. He does great for his men, but if a girl isn't into fun and games, he sends her out to just enough auditions and for bad jobs."

"He's never made a pass at me," I said, indignantly.

"He probably has." He went back to His plate. "You've just missed it, is all."

"Well, there's got to be at least one honest agent out there," I grumbled.

He looked at me with a guilty smile. "Yeah, Diogenes, there are a few."

"Well, why don't you recommend one, Phillip," said Mrs. Sperling with a sly grin.

He smiled at her. "Um. She could try Shelly Carson, at the Talent Company."

"I thought you didn't like her," said Mrs. Sperling.

"Okay, she gets more money out of me than I want to spend." He smiled at me again. "Sometimes there are more important things than budgets." He got up and wiped His mouth. "I gotta run, Aunt Delilah."

"Off to cast your new film?" She smiled as He kissed her cheek.

"That's tomorrow. And it's a video."

"That's right. I had forgotten."

During that time, my heart took a diving leap to my feet. If He was casting a video, there were good odds He needed dancers. And there I was, selling Him on my friend instead of me. Not that I begrudged Tina the sell. I just could have spent some time on me, too.

He turned that wonderful smile on me then fled. I melted and forgave Him for every time He wouldn't cast me.

Mrs. Sperling only waited long enough for the door to shut.

"My dear Donna, it would appear to me that you are completely infatuated with Phillip."

"Fat lot of good it's going to do me. I can't even put in a plug for myself."

"There, there. Don't give up hope yet. If you're finished eating, hurry and clean up, and call that Shelley Carson. Tell her you can bring her a picture and resume today. Then bring the V.W. around. I'm in a top-down mood, and we've got other errands to run, too."

"Just because I was divorcing the man doesn't mean I wanted the asshole dead," Ramona Bistler swore vehemently.

She was scared. About average height, she had dark hair that had been streaked, high cheekbones and a wraith-like figure dressed in a faded designer denim mini and a fuchsia silk blouse. Her tights were fuchsia also, and she wore multi-colored ankle-high leather boots. She paced about her Laura Ashley living room, puffing on a cigarette.

"Why would I jump to that conclusion?" asked Mrs. Sperling.

"You're here, aren't you?" She waved the hand holding her smoke, sprinkling ash in a wide arc. "Come on, Delilah. You wouldn't want to talk to me unless I was a suspect."

"I would guess, Ms. Bistler, that your friends have been frightening you needlessly. Your closeness to the victim makes you a good source of information. That is why I am here. I'm certainly not about to classify anybody as a suspect with as many questions unanswered as there currently are. Just so I can eliminate you, what were you doing the night your husband died?"

"Nothing. I... Well, I was alone all night. I took a short drive because I felt like it, then came here and watched T.V. until I went to bed." She sighed. "It doesn't look good, does it? And no, there wasn't anybody who could have seen me."

"Are you sure? Did you make any stops? Even a mundane stop at the grocery for cigarettes or even for gas for your car."

"None. My maid stocks plenty of cigarettes for me, and Steve, my chauffeur, sees to keeping plenty of gas in the tank. I suppose I should say, my former chauffeur. I fired him yesterday." She stubbed out her cigarette in the overflowing ashtray next to her sofa.

"Why?"

"Insubordination, for starters, and the bastard was stealing from me. I needed him to get through the funeral, but after that, I fired him."

"Did he know you were about to?"

"I hadn't mentioned it to anyone. He seemed pretty shocked when I told him. And pissed off."

"Indeed. Do you have his home address, and may I have it?"

"I think my lawyer has all that. He takes care of all my financial matters. He's Eugene Montoinne, over on Sunset. Nine thousand something or other. You know, those big towers where all the agents' offices are?"

I knew the buildings she meant, rather better than I wished to admit.

Mrs. Sperling nodded. "If you would be so kind

as to call him and let him know we'll be coming, it would be appreciated."

Bistler walked over to the other end table and picked up the handset to one of those real fancy old-fashioned phones. Not the upright kind with the part you speak into on the base and the earpiece is separate, but the other kind. Anyway, she got through right away and told the person on the other end to answer any questions Mrs. Sperling might have.

"That's settled," she said, hanging up. "Any other questions?"

"Yes. Did your husband belong to a gymnasium or health club of some sort?"

"Of course. The same one I belong to. It's on Santa Monica."

"Near the Rodeo district, or closer in to downtown?"

"Close to Rodeo."

"That fits in perfectly. This may seem a rather personal question, but what did your husband wear to bed?"

"To bed? With me?" Bistler fidgeted with her cigarette. "Um. Nothing. If you want the complete truth, Josh was a bore, from the first day to the last. He was a nice person. But he was the worst stick in the mud I've ever known. All he cared about was that damn gallery. The only parties he went to were connected to the gallery, and he didn't go to many of those. The more established he got, the fewer parties he went to."

"But what did he wear when he wasn't with

you?"

Bistler hesitated. "I... Shit, I don't know. We weren't exactly a close couple. He kept to himself mostly, and I didn't butt in. I'm a night person, anyway, and he's the morning type. For two people who lived in the same house, we didn't see much of each other."

"Why did you marry him?"

Bistler laughed. "Why else? For his money."

"Was he aware of that?"

"Beats me. I couldn't have cared less if he did. I only wanted to stay married long enough to get a good settlement. It was all part of my game plan. First, I had to get a guy like Josh, who could be counted on to ignore me. Then I had to get him to marry me, wait a few years until I had a good case, then sue him for divorce and get as much money as I could. In the meantime, I stashed away some more cash in a Swiss account, so if I couldn't get a decent alimony, my butt would still be covered and comfortable." She stopped and examined Mrs. Sperling. "It was heartless, I know. But I couldn't afford feelings. I grew up dirt poor. That's why I came to L.A. I was gonna be rich or die trying. I really wanted to be in the movies. Was that ever a joke. Nailing a rich husband was a lot easier. As soon as I had a few million in the bank, I told Josh goodbye. Kicked him out two weeks ago today. And this is his house. I'd do it again in a minute."

"You were certainly motivated," replied Mrs. Sperling without a hint of judgment.

"Not enough to kill him. There are things even

I won't do."

"Of course. Is it safe to assume you didn't share a bedroom?"

"We didn't. Actually, Josh played right into my hands on that one. About six months after we were married, Josh asked me to take my own room because I was so prone to staying up late, and he didn't like being wakened up when I finally went to bed."

"May I see the room?"

"Sure. I was going to have the maid clean it out this afternoon. The police haven't released the stuff from the gallery yet."

The room was kind of dark, and very neat, perfectly fitting what we knew of Mr. Stein's personality. After I described it, Mrs. Sperling had me go through the closet and chest of drawers.

"It's the same sort of stuff that was in the police report," I said. "Not as much. Looks like he took the bulk of his stuff when he left. There's only a couple pairs of pants, three shirts, some sweaters." I opened the chest. "I don't see any undershorts. Hey, look at this. Two pairs of pajamas. They look really fancy." I handed a pair to Mrs. Sperling.

"Silk," she observed. "Are there any other pairs?"

I hurried through the drawers. "Nope. Not much else here, either. He took all his shoes and belts. About the only thing he left was eight suits."

"That's interesting," Mrs. Sperling nodded. "It would appear Mr. Stein did not like dressing up."

Bistler had nothing to say because she had shown us the room and left.

I checked under the bed just to be thorough. "Nothing under the bed. Do you want to take the room apart?"

"No. I don't think we're going to find anything revealing here."

I ran my hand between the mattress and box springs.

"You're probably right. I don't see any signs of counterfeiting."

"That would take a great deal more space than is in this room. We'll go finish speaking with Ms. Bistler."

We returned to the living room where Bistler smoked and paced.

"Ms. Bistler, did your husband have a studio in the house?"

She snorted. "Josh was no artist. Couldn't even draw stick figures."

"That's odd. I believe there were rumors going around that he was counterfeiting artworks."

"Could be." Bistler shrugged. "If he was, someone else was doing the work. I heard the rumors, too. It doesn't sound like Josh, him being such a bore and all. But I wouldn't be surprised."

"Did he ever give you any indication he was?"

"Josh gave me no indication of anything he was doing. I didn't really care, either. As long as the money came in, I didn't give a damn what he did."

"Have you seen the terms of his will?"

"Yes." Bistler paced even more frenetically. "Would you believe he left everything to me? Does not sound good, does it?"

"It's not an unusual way to dispose of one's money. Do you know of anyone who might have had something against your husband?"

"Oh, come on! I didn't even know his friends. How am I supposed to know his enemies?"

"Maybe you've heard rumors."

She shrugged and lit another cigarette. "Maybe one of his competitors. That gallery did a good business."

"That is an angle I didn't think of."

"The cops sure did."

"Have the police spoken to you since you identified your husband's body?"

"Yesterday. What's his name, Michaelson? He came over asking where I was that night and about enemies. I told him what I told you."

"Excellent. Well, I'd better not trouble you anymore, Ms. Bistler. Thank you very much for your information."

We left, much to Bistler's relief. Our first stop was her lawyer's office. The receptionist sent us back almost immediately. Mr. Montoinne was a fairly short man, balding, and dressed in the required dark pin-stripe three-piece suit. He looked to be as honest and humble a family retainer as one could want.

"Good afternoon, Mrs. Sperling," he said with sincere warmth. But something about him didn't feel right to me. "It's a pleasure to finally meet you. Your reputation is outstanding."

"Thank you, Mr. Montoinne." Mrs. Sperling graciously took the seat she was offered. Eleanor curled up at her feet. I was left ignored and standing by the door. "What I came for was an address that your client, Ms. Ramona Bistler, said you had."

"The chauffeur's. Yes. My secretary is digging it out now."

"Then while we're waiting, would you mind answering a few questions?"

"My pleasure." He scurried around his huge oak desk and sat down.

"How long have you been retained by Ms. Bistler?"

"For about two and a half years. Her late husband recommended me when she wanted someone to deal with some investments for her."

"Why not a regular stockbroker?"

"Part of it was the legal awkwardness of maintaining separate ownership. California's divorce laws are such that anything acquired during the term of the marriage is considered community property unless there is a special contract drawn up. Mr. Stein had made some gifts of cash to his wife, and she wanted to invest them, and at the same time maintain sole ownership of the funds and whatever profit from them against the possibility of a divorce. She was also afraid Mr. Stein's attorney would be biased in his favor, so at her husband's suggestion, she retained me. Through power of attorney, I eventually became responsible for managing her household affairs, including retaining an accountant, hiring her staff, and seeing to it they were paid, overseeing her stockbroker, details like that."

"So, you are well informed as to her financial status."

"Intimately so."

Mrs. Sperling's eyebrow lifted. "Interesting choice of words."

"You are referring to Ms. Bistler's reputation?" Mr. Montoinne leered slightly. "With her promiscuous tendencies, it's not at all surprising. And I can see you asking yourself if I have... Well, gone beyond the usual bounds of attorney-client relations."

"I blush to confess the thought did cross my mind."

"You're blushing in this town? Mrs. Sperling, I am a man, and Ramona Bistler does have a way about her."

"I get the point. We needn't be salacious."

"Your good breeding shows. I don't run into much of that anymore. It's a pleasant change."

"Thank you. To return to my original line of questioning, being so knowledgeable about Ms. Bistler's assets, perhaps you could confirm the existence of a Swiss bank account in her name and give me a rough estimate of the amount therein."

"She has one in Zurich. If she continues investing at her current rate, she should be able to better her standard of living on the interest alone."

"That's a great deal of money. Is she aware of

that?"

"I would say not. I have yet to tell her the exact figures, beyond mentioning that she needn't be concerned about her settlement. Fortunately, I do not need to inform the court about the Swiss bank account, since those assets cannot be recognized. Or I wouldn't have had to. But some caution had to be exercised regarding her investments, on the odd chance the judge developed sympathy for Mr. Stein, and imposed an alimony payment on her. For that reason, I purposely kept her in the dark regarding her assets, thus making it harder for her to perjure herself on the witness stand."

"You thought she might?"

"I didn't want to give her the opportunity. And being aware of her tendencies, I also strongly recommended she refrain from adulterous liaisons, or at least be extremely discreet about them so as not to give her husband a case against her, which in turn could result in a minimal settlement or in her paying alimony. It's all a moot point now. Her husband left her everything."

"What are the odds of his family fighting the will?"

"Fair to middling, I would guess. They've got plenty themselves, or so I hear. But that doesn't mean they're generous. A lot depends on how they feel about my client. That's the reason I have strongly recommended that she avoid overt romantic liaisons with men for the time being."

"Have you heard anything regarding her husband's gallery?"

"I never paid any attention to it, to be honest, beyond sending my son there for his Niedeman serigraphs."

"He has an HN4?"

"I have no idea."

"If he does, I would suggest having it authenticated. There's a possibility someone switched counterfeits for Mr. Stein's genuine ones. And could you please call me with the results?" Mrs. Sperling reached into her purse and removed a small leather case. "Here is one of my cards." She stood as she handed it to him. "I appreciate the way you took time out of your busy schedule to speak with me."

"It was my pleasure, Mrs. Sperling." Mr. Montoinne was up and around his desk in a second. "If there is anything I can do for you in the future, please do not hesitate to call."

"I won't, Mr. Montoinne."

I opened the door and we left, stopping only to get Steve Lansky's address from the secretary.

"Where next?" I asked as Eleanor jumped into the back seat of the Bug convertible. "Mr. Lansky's?"

"Not yet." Mrs. Sperling tied a scarf around her hair. "I'd like to speak with Sergeant Michaelson before he goes home today." She got into the passenger seat next to me. "I don't believe we're far from there anyway."

"It's what? Four o'clock?" I snapped on my seatbelt. "We should be able to get there pretty quick."

"And where is Mr. Lansky's address?"

"Studio City."

"Good heavens. We'll end up on the freeway during rush hour. We'll just see Sergeant Michaelson."

"Fine." The VW caught immediately, and I backed out of the parking space. Mr. Montoinne's secretary had validated our parking ticket and we got out of there without any money left behind.

In spite of a quick ride over there, Sergeant Michaelson was getting ready to go when we arrived.

"I knew it," he grinned ruefully. "I knew I'd never make it out of here early."

"Is it urgent, Sergeant?" asked Mrs. Sperling. "I can always return tomorrow morning."

"Nah. I take it you want the latest on the Stein murder."

"It would help."

"Okay. What do you know about a Steven Lansky?"

"Ms. Ramona Bistler's chauffeur, or former chauffeur. He told Donna that Ms. Bistler spent the night of Mr. Stein's death joyriding, and later filled the tank of her car to cover up her trip."

"Before or after he was fired?"

"Before."

"That lends even more credence to his story, which was basically the same, except with an even stronger implication that Ms. Bistler was involved in her husband's death. I, however, spoke to him after he was fired, trying to confirm Ms. Bistler's story that she was home alone after a brief drive."

Mrs. Sperling nodded. "She seems to be keeping her story straight fairly well."

"Ah-hah. You think she's lying."

"So do you."

Sergeant Michaelson laughed. "I got one on you, Mrs. Sperling. I know she is. After hearing Lansky's story, I spent a good day and a half checking out gas stations in the near vicinity of Ramona Bistler's home. It was a long shot."

"All the more satisfying when it pays off." Mrs. Sperling smiled, as anxious as a kid on Christmas Eve. "What did you find?"

"That Ms. Ramona Bistler did indeed fill her tank with gasoline around eleven-thirty on the night her husband died. She paid for it with a charge card, so there's a written record of it. And the station attendant particularly remembers her because her engine died just as she pulled in, and they had to push the car to the pump. Her tank was completely empty."

"Very supportive of our current theory, but for one thing."

"What?" Michaelson groaned.

"I'm not sure about the theory."

"Keep plugging, then. And don't worry about Bistler. It's pretty suspicious, but not enough to arrest her on. We need a lot more evidence."

"Too true. Still, it was a fortunate discovery, Sergeant."

Michaelson chuckled. "That's not all we discovered. It didn't get in the initial report because the lab boys didn't get to it until Friday, but they found something a little odd in the gallery, itself."

"They did?" Mrs. Sperling's eyebrow lifted.

"Yeah. There were about five prints stacked in a corner with a note that said they weren't for sale." Michaelson flipped through his notepad. "A Yamagata, two Sumners, and two Niedemans. We got them authenticated."

"And..?"

"All of them were fakes."

Mrs. Sperling nodded. "Then Mr. Stein knew about the counterfeiting. Thank you for sharing all that with me. I'll organize my notes this evening and send them over first thing tomorrow morning."

"Thanks a lot, Mrs. Sperling. I'd better get going. My wife thinks I'm on the way."

"Give her my regards and tell her I'd like to have you and the family to dinner soon."

"I'm sure she'll look forward to it. See you around."

We left the office, but not the building. Mrs. Sperling's contacts with the police are pretty good. We spent an hour and a half on the firing range. The idea, of course, was not to use the gun at all. Mrs. Sperling makes a point of confronting her criminals in such a way that they can't use violence. But criminals being criminals, they don't always make that an option.

ack at the house, I hung up the phone and gazed at Mrs. Sperling thoughtfully. She worked quietly on a crewel sampler. We'd just finished dinner and were relaxing in the living room.

"That was Shelley Carson just now," I told Mrs. Sperling. "She says she'll take me on and is sending me out tomorrow on an audition."

"How nice," Mrs. Sperling said innocently.

"Funny. It just happens to be for a video directed by Phillip DuPre."

"Are you implying something?"

"I don't know." I sunk into the sofa. "I feel like I'm being set up."

Mrs. Sperling chuckled. "Assuming you are, it's not the sort of set up I'd complain about if I were you."

"I suppose. It doesn't seem fair to the other dancers, though. And I can't help wondering if there isn't supposed to be some sort of payback, if you know what I mean."

"Your career is in no position for you to be worrying about being fair to other dancers, my dear. Furthermore, Phillip is perfectly capable of keeping his personal and professional biases separate. As for the payback, don't even think of it. Phillip was well raised in a good home, and it shows."

"Hmm." I thought for a few minutes. "You wouldn't happen to know if, uh, Mr. DuPre has a girlfriend?"

Mrs. Sperling laughed. "Donna, I'm afraid you're on your own as far as that's concerned. I refuse to meddle." She paused. "But Phillip is not seeing anyone at the moment."

"Well, it's not going to make any difference. Like I'm really going to say anything."

"It might not be a bad idea." She absorbed herself in her stitchery.

"Yeah. Right." I got up and stretched. "I'm just a peon dancer hyphen chauffeur. He sure is gorgeous, though."

And nice, with no ego. It was hopeless. I went to bed.

The next morning, I made a quick run past the Beverly Hills police station before class. I worked out extra hard, so I was dragging a little when I made it back to the house. Mrs. Sperling had me join her for brunch, poached eggs with Benedictine sauce, fresh steamed broccoli, and fresh fruit with cream.

"You sound worn out." Mrs. Sperling smiled softly at me.

"I am a little. I got your notes in, before class even. That Willoughby guy said he'd bring them to Michaelson."

"Thank you. Speaking of that, I don't believe you ever told me the results of your adventure Monday night."

"Oh, that." I recounted my conversation with the bartender at Hennessey's. "I also forgot to tell you I dropped by the police station the next morning. They were waiting for me. It turns out Fred Gonzagos did a small stretch for forgery with intent to fraud six years back. He got out three years ago and has supposedly stayed clean since. More like he hasn't gotten caught. They listed an Anita Llanez as his sister. I wrote the address down somewhere." I dug through my dance bag. "Here it is. It's in Montebello."

"Quite a distance. I'll try to contact her by phone. While I do, why don't you rest a little? I assume you want to be fresh for your audition this afternoon."

"Yeah." I sighed and sat back in my chair.

"Feeling nervous?" Her smile was a little sly.

"It's an audition. Of course, I'm nervous. I don't know. It just feels strange, is all. But like you say, I'm in no position to complain."

She nodded.

"Mrs. Sperling, can I ask you a question?"

"Of course."

"Why are you helping me develop a career that is going to cause me to leave you?" I winced a little as I asked.

She hesitated. "Because of how hard I fought to realize my dream of becoming a detective. I fought tooth and nail to get the state to let me test for my investigator's license. Almost took them to court. And it was years before anyone gave me any credit for my skills. It was so painful to know how good I was, and yet not be taken seriously because I was supposedly handicapped. For similar reasons, it's much the same for most young artists. You know you're a good dancer and actress, but no one recognizes it, and no one will take you seriously until you make tremendous amounts of money. Even then some people won't. Poor Jimmy felt so bad because his family considered his writing a nice hobby until his first book hit the Bestseller list. It's a wonderful book, and it had gotten twenty-eight rejection slips before I talked to a friend of my father's who's a literary agent. My detecting was a nice hobby, also, and nobody would believe that I could be any good at it. Finally, my father convinced a friend of his that I might be able to tell whether or not a burglary the police considered just a standard break-in was indeed more than it seemed. It was a murder attempt based on an old grudge that I was able to ferret out. I saved that friend's life. He thanked me and told me he would tell his friends about me on one condition."

"What was that?"

"That I promise that if I ever came across another struggling dreamer, I would help him or her achieve that dream. You see, someone had done the same for him, and made him make the same promise. It was such a noble goal, he thought it best to carry it on. And I have."

"I think I will, too." I grinned. "If I get anywhere. There aren't enough nice people in the world."

"Maybe we can change that."

We were on the road by noon. Our first stop was the security company. The guard we wanted was still out sick. The supervisor did let us see his report. We saw for ourselves that nothing suspicious was seen. Then we stopped at a second gallery near Mr. Stein's.

A tall, light-haired young man loudly held court at a desk in the middle of the store. He had a phone to one ear and talked to a pair of well-dressed matrons and another trendily dressed man.

"Hal, get a good look at that sculpture and tell me it isn't the hottest thing in years," the young man directed. The other man gazed moodily at an abstract plastic contortion of some kind. "Ladies, I'm telling you, the blue frames on those prints. Joe, you're back. Get your tickets and get out here. That show is going to be the biggest thing this season... You are really gonna regret it, I promise you. Ladies, would I lie to you? The blue frames. Hal, that is the sculpture you want. I'm telling you. Don't buy it and you'll live to regret it."

"I think I'd live to regret owning it," I whispered to Mrs. Sperling. "It's plastic and it looks like it's in pain."

"That's probably the point. Are there any other sculptures here?"

"Yeah." I took her elbow and guided her to a small bronze on a free-standing white carpeted box.

"Lady, lady, don't handle the merchandise!" yelped the young man. "Joe, there won't be any selection by the time the show gets out to you. Those pieces are going like hotcakes."

"I'm sorry, sir. I should have asked," Mrs. Sperling answered. "Would it be possible? I have no other way of observing it."

"Oh." He spotted Eleanor. "I s'pose. Be careful. Maybe the puce, ladies, but I'm telling you, the blue's better. Joe, you're nuts. Come on, for me? Are you gonna buy it, Hal, or not?"

In answer, Hal waved and left. The young man cursed him softly.

"The plastic?" Mrs. Sperling asked me. "And what does he look like?"

I took her over to the piece. "Tall, with dishwater blonde hair. The plastic is red, the same color and subtlety as a fire engine on a three-alarm fire."

"Ooph! It wouldn't go in my home at all."

The two ladies abandoned the gallery and the young man found himself hanging up.

"Well, ladies, how are you today?"

"Quite well, thank you," Mrs. Sperling answered. "You are...?"

"Edgar Hendricks."

"Mr. Hendricks, I would like to speak with the owner of the gallery."

"It's your lucky day, ma'am, I am he. Let me tell you about this sculpture."

"I'm afraid it would be grossly out of place in

my home."

"Personally, I can't stand it, either."

Mrs. Sperling's eyebrow lifted. "The hottest thing in years?"

Eleanor sniffed at the base. If she'd been a male, I would have worried.

"For the right people, like Hal. He's into trendy. You, ma'am, are much more interested in something of more lasting value."

"Actually, I'm interested in Mr. Stein's gallery."

"That's closed. He, uh, passed away. He didn't carry much sculpture anyway. I've got a piece over here that I'm telling you, you want."

I guided Mrs. Sperling to Hendricks' pride. She graciously put her hands on it.

"I'd heard rumors Mr. Stein had been selling counterfeit art," she said, feeling a polished wood carving that resembled a twisted blob.

"Everyone's heard that one," said Hendricks. "Can't prove it, of course."

"I wonder who started it."

"I don't give a damn. Stein's out of my way, and so much the better. He was what you call supercilious. Biggest snob in town. Too good to go to anybody's parties."

"I take it your business did much better than his."

"Well, yeah! Hell, yes!"

"I can imagine." Mrs. Sperling did not believe him for a second. "What were you doing a week ago tonight?"

"Me? Let's see. I locked up, and I... What did I

do? Oh yeah. I went to Emil's for a bite to eat and hung around the bar there all evening. Picked up on a chick and brought her home."

While Mrs. Sperling and Hendricks were conversing, I wandered around. I noticed that his very large computer monitor was on, and a spreadsheet was splayed across it. Keeping one eye on Hendricks, I read his store's financial history for the past six months. Then I wandered away. Mrs. Sperling convinced Hendricks that she really didn't want the wood blob and we left.

"I get the feeling you don't believe Hendricks was doing better than the late Mr. Stein," I said, pulling the Lexus into traffic.

"Not for one minute."

"What would you say if I could prove it?" I grinned.

"Donna, you didn't do anything illegal?"

"I don't think so. Borderline at worst. The spreadsheet was on his desktop monitor and not minimized or anything. I just looked. They won't be able to trace it to me anyway because I just looked."

"What did you find?"

"Hendricks has been operating in the red since July, and he wasn't doing too well then."

"Which means unless Mr. Stein was doing worse, a very unlikely situation, Mr. Hendricks has every reason to be pleased by Mr. Stein's death."

"Which he as good as said he was." I checked the rearview mirror and changed lanes. "Looks like we've got another suspect."

"Even more interesting, he fits the description of Dolores' friend who sold her the Niedemans, and Mr. Hendricks would have access to wholesale prints."

"But why dump them on Dolores when he could sell them at his store at a much higher markup?"

"What if he got them by dishonest means?"

"That makes sense. Where to now?"

"Let's investigate the building where Mr. Stein's gallery is." Mrs. Sperling got that vague look on her face. "There's something going on there, but I can't quite put my finger on it."

I went ahead and parked in Mr. Stein's space behind the gallery, mostly because I knew he wouldn't be using it. We went around front to the foyer, though. According to the directory next to the elevator, there were four offices in the building, but only one of them was occupied. We took the elevator up to the third floor, confirmed that those two offices were empty, then walked down to the second floor.

The second office there was empty. But the one closest to the front of the building still had an occupant for the moment, at any rate. "Best Rentals," proclaimed the sign on the glass door, with the website address underneath. There was a man on the other side snarling as he glared at his computer.

He was fairly hefty and wearing a heavy wool sweater and gloves with the fingers cut off. It seemed a little extreme except that the building was still pretty chilly. He looked up and glared at us as we walked into the office.

"Can I help you?" he asked more out of duty than interest as we walked in.

"I'm hoping you can help us," Mrs. Sperling said with a smile. "We're investigating the death of Mr. Josh Stein."

The man shook his head. "Never heard of him."

"He was your downstairs neighbor," Mrs. Sperling said.

"You mean the gallery?" The man shrugged. "Huh. Didn't pay much attention to it. But if he was murdered, you might look at the building's owners."

"Why?"

"Simple. They're trying to squeeze us out of here so they can jack up the rental rates." The man held up his sweater. "See this?"

"I'm afraid not." Mrs. Sperling smiled.

The man's eyebrows raised as he realized his mistake. "Shit. I'm sorry. I didn't notice. Anyway, I'm sitting here bundled up like a fucking Inuit because there's no frickin' heat in this building. And no AC, either, in the summer. New owners came in last year and it has been fucking miserable since. They must be forcing us out. We lost three tenants in the past six months. I'm only here because my lease isn't up until next month."

"That sounds most unpleasant."

"I wouldn't put it past them to kill that gallery guy. They'll sink to no end to get more money out of us."

Mrs. Sperling smiled sympathetically. "It does sound like it. Well, pray excuse us for interrupting your day."

We left quickly, although we took our time getting down that spiral staircase.

"So, do we have a new suspect?" I asked as we headed to the car.

"I seriously doubt it," Mrs. Sperling said. "The new owners may be trying to force the old tenants out. It does happen. But I find it hard to believe they would think it in their best interests to murder one."

"That makes sense." I sighed. "Where next?"

"Mr. Stein's gymnasium."

Thanks to the magic of GPS, I found it easily enough. It was one of those really posh clubs with carpet that you sink to your ankles in, and good-looking desk clerks in tailored blouses and skirts who take your I.D. and exchange it for their own keys to their lockers. Mrs. Sperling asked for the club manager, a Bernice Lockwell. She was busy at that moment. We were invited to sit in the lobby, next to the pro shop, an open area filled with racks of leotards, skimpy tops, and skimpier bottoms.

I happen to have a body that does well in very high French cut bottoms, as long as I have a belt. I'm too long for a single leotard without something breaking it up. While we waited, I looked through the clothes, hoping to find a gorgeous and sexy ensemble for my audition. It was for jazz dancers, and Carson had said wear high-heeled dance shoes. I might still have worn my traditional black ballet leotard and sheer skirt, except He was going to be there. I wanted to look a little sexy. I mean, if He was going to be hanging around Mrs. Sperling, anyway... You never know.

Miss Lockwell showed up just then and brought me down to earth.

"I understand Mr. Joshua Stein was a member here," Mrs. Sperling said after introducing herself and me.

"Yes. We much regret his passing," replied Miss Lockwell, a thin, bland corporate type with light blonde hair.

"Did he keep a permanent locker here?"

"As a matter of fact, he did. I wish I could show it to you, but that's not allowed. And it's already been cleared out."

"By whom? And when?"

"A youngish man, light-haired, and fairly tall. I don't think he gave his name. He had a note from Mr. Stein's widow giving him permission to clear the locker. He came by earlier this afternoon."

"Do you have a copy of the note?"

Miss Lockwell blushed. "I'm sorry. I had intended to keep and file it, but during our conversation, the young man must have gotten it back and kept it himself. It's the only explanation I can think of. I can't find the note anywhere."

"Somehow, it doesn't surprise me." Mrs. Sperling smiled with chagrin. "Thank you very much, Miss Lockwell. Let's go, Donna."

Mrs. Sperling remained preoccupied all the

way out to the car.

"That guy that cleared out the locker," I said as I started the engine. "He fits the description, too."

"I noticed. The aggravating thing is I've been given to understand a lot of young men in Southern California are light-haired and tall."

"There are a lot of them. Where to?"

"What time is it? One thirty?"

"One forty-five."

"Melrose Avenue, and that designer's store. Devonaire, I believe."

The store was in a basic, boring white two-story building. The sign looked like it came straight from Times Square. It was a big black, rectangle, framed by chaser lights. The name, "Devonaire,"flashed on the top half, and a host of existentialist quotes crawled along the bottom half. The store, itself, was half-way normal.

It had a white interior, with light pine shelving, and the displays were spare and uncluttered as if Devon didn't need a lot of stock to make money. He probably didn't. The prices were incredible.

The clothes were nice, though. He had several knit jumpsuits with stirrup legs, in olives and golds. The dresses were similar colors, but straight sheaths with long sleeves and a variety of back openings and collars, made out of heavy linen.

As we walked in, a clerk folded sweaters with the most wonderful designs on them. The clerk's blonde hair had been clipped close to their head, except on top, where it stood up straight. They wore no make-up, and their jaw was masculine. They were at least six feet tall and broad-shouldered. But their hands were small and feminine, and the skin-tight body suit clung to two bumps on their chest.

"Is there a clerk?" Mrs. Sperling asked softly.

"Uh, yeah."

"Excuse me, might we see the owner?" Mrs. Sperling said a bit louder.

The clerk looked at us and jerked their head towards the back. We went past them to the dressing rooms, which were stalls with canvas curtains for doors.

The young man was in complete contrast to the clerk. His hair was black and long, and he wore a black Nehru jacket over black 501 jeans. He couldn't have been more than five-five.

"I am Devon," he announced with an extremely New York accent. "Welcome to my humble establishment." He came over and shook our hands. "I'm so glad to see you ladies. And a doggie. I just love poochies." Eleanor looked at him but accepted the head-scratching as her due. "I know. I know. You're just browsing. Be my guest. Let's get to know each other. Don't worry. You're in my hands. I will find just the right look for you. Gillian, find these beautiful ladies a glass of wine."

"Thank you very much, Mr. Devon," said Mrs. Sperling.

"Oh, please call me Devon. Everybody does."

"Very well. I'd actually like to ask you a question or two."

"Ask on, ask on. I'm an open book."

Gillian, the clerk, pressed a glass of white wine into my hand. I sniffed at it. It wasn't bad.

"Thank you," said Mrs. Sperling. She didn't drink hers. "Devon, I understand you knew Mr. Joshua Stein."

"Oh, lord. For years. We've known each other since we were babes practically."

"And how long would that be?"

"Let's see, I came out here, what, four years ago. I had a fling with Jeff, then there was Thomas. Oh, yeah. I met Josh when I was dating Earl. Christmas two years ago."

"I see. I was told you had a disagreement with Mr. Stein a week ago today."

"Of course, we did." Devon laughed. "Josh and I, we're always tiffing. Last Wednesday was nothing."

"There was a piece of pottery lost."

"Oh, don't tell me, you're here about the insurance. I told Josh I'd pay for it. I called him up that night. Listen, don't even worry about it. Or would you rather I paid the company? Honest, I'll pay for it. It's no big deal."

"What were you arguing about?"

"Silly stuff. I get excited, you know? But Josh has a wonderful gallery. It's over in Beverly Hills. Wait a minute, you've already been out there. Of course, you have, for the claim, right? Isn't it marvelous? He's got the most wonderful pieces. Did you see that beautiful abstract by Winston Seever? It's incredible."

Mrs. Sperling pressed her lips together. "I'm afraid I didn't."

"Oh, check it out the next time you're in. It is simply wonderful."

"Regarding Wednesday, where were you that evening?"

"Oh, nightclubbing. The usual. I'm all over the place. Where were you? Or does it make any difference? Do you nightclub? I know the most incredible hot spot."

"Were you there Wednesday?"

"I told you, I'm everywhere."

"What time did you say you called Mr. Stein."

"I don't believe I did!" Devon giggled. "Oh, hell, it was nine o'clock, ten o'clock, eleven o'clock, somewhere in there. Ask Josh. He could tell you. Or is he trying to say I didn't call? He'd do that. Trust me, I did. Why would I say I did when I didn't, because I am going to pay for that pottery. I mean I'd be stupid to say I told him I'd pay for it if I wasn't going to. That man is such a stick in the mud. But has he got a great gallery."

"Well, thank you very much, Devon." Mrs. Sperling turned, then stopped. "I just thought, where was Mr. Stein when you called him?"

"Where else? His home. He closes the place at six, on the dot. Are you leaving already?"

"It's been very pleasant, but we have other appointments."

"I'll bet you do. Well, come back soon. We'll get you something nice to try on. Gillian, take these glasses."

Devon escorted us out with a running monologue on how nice we were, how great Josh was, and how nice it would be to see us again. Mrs. Sperling let out a sigh of relief when we got back to the car.

"He's a character," I said.

"Home, Donna. I can't take much more of this."

I chuckled. "At least he didn't assume you were handicapped."

"It's amazing what people don't notice. And that's the second time today."

"Well, you don't wear sunglasses, and you don't carry a white cane. He must have figured you had Eleanor in a harness for a different purpose."

Mrs. Sperling frowned. "He didn't tell us anything, either."

"That's right. He didn't. And he lied about Wednesday night. Or did he? The coroner's report said Stein died between eight and two, or something like that."

"He also said that Mr. Stein was at home when he called. It's possible Mr. Stein led Devon to believe he was at home when he wasn't. But if Mr. Stein was at the house, then Ms. Bistler has some explaining to do."

I gasped. "He kept talking as if Stein was alive."

"I noticed. That is easily managed."

"That's still another suspect. How many possibles do we have?"

"Well, there's Fred Gonzagos. He has no real motive visible, but possible because of a suspicious disappearance, compounded by suspicious remarks made the last time he was seen. Until we find him, nothing much can be learned there. Then there's Ramona Bistler. She took a mysterious drive the night of her husband's death that she lied about, and she has a substantial motive on several levels. And of course, Devon. No known motive beyond a vague argument, although I did get the impression he was less fond of Mr. Stein than he wanted us to believe."

"But Devon is short and dark. Wait. Gillian isn't. They're tall and blonde, too."

"They?"

"Gender neutral," I said. "But definitely tall enough and masculine enough to count."

"Hm. There is that to consider. We also have Edgar Hendricks. He, too, fits the description of a mysterious young man known to be selling potentially stolen prints possibly belonging to Mr. Stein, and known to have removed possible evidence. We should confirm that note. The only problem is we can't trust the veracity of the only person who can confirm it. We should also confirm Mr. Hendricks' whereabouts the night of the murder before it gets too much later, and memories get dimmer. I'm afraid, Donna, I'm going to have to send you bar hopping again tonight."

"Oo. Emil's is expensive."

Mrs. Sperling chuckled. "Get Phillip to take you."

"What?" My jaw dropped. "Are you kidding? I can barely get out a complete sentence when he's around. He's not going to want to go out with a peon like me, anyway."

"Don't sell yourself short."

"Oh, come on, Mrs. Sperling. A nobody dancer and he can go out with major players? In my dreams."

"I could ask him for you, if you like."

"Don't you dare!"

"If you insist, I won't. But please see that you are accompanied."

"I will."

looked good when I went to that audition. My hair was up in a long, curled ponytail. My make-up had all the highlights I could get away with. I wore my sexiest leotard, a shimmery gray one with narrow straps, a diving back, and leg holes cut up to my elbows. My tights were a shimmery neutral color that matched my tan dance shoes. My black leg warmers had flecks of silver in them.

I did not look that hot on the way there. It was cold and close to sunset. To keep warm, I had on my rip-stop pants and my beat-up jacket. But the only person who would see me in those was the girl at the sign in sheet.

She was bored, as usual, and showed me into the warm-up studio.

"Here's the last one," she said.

"Fine," said the choreographer. He was a short, dumpy little guy I'd seen many times before and had yet to learn his name. "You've got five minutes to warm up."

I noticed he wasn't talking to just me, but also to the other fifteen people in the room. I stripped down, put my pants and jacket in my dance bag, changed from my running shoes to my dance shoes, and pulled out a shimmery, sheer dance skirt.

"Donna's dressed to kill," laughed a familiar voice as I tied the skirt around me.

"Mickey!" I yelped. I bounded over and kissed him.

"Donna! Thank God, they called you." Tina came over and hugged me. "I swear, if they hadn't, I was going to go straight over and bounce your agent on his ear. You're looking good. You must have heard who's directing this thing. You know, that babe of all babes, Phillip DuPre."

"Uh, yeah, I heard."

"Rats," said Mickey. "I thought she was breathing heavy because of me."

"Shut up, Dooley." Tina slugged him in the arm.

We all three warmed up, stretching out our muscles, bouncing about.

"Alright," the choreographer boomed out. "I'll be teaching you the audition. When you get inside, they'll work with you. Everybody get partners, male/female, please."

I grabbed Mickey. Tina didn't mind. She had an equally good partner. It was a tough routine. After four run-throughs, it looked like we all had it.

A wave of dancers flowed into the studio from the taping room. As they abated, Phillip DuPre appeared, talking to someone in the room.

"Why don't you start running through it?" He said. "I've got a phone call to make."

He turned into the studio and spotted me. I froze. He smiled at me, then the others then pulled his iPhone out of his pants pocket and dialed.

Tina nudged me. "There he is. The Phillip DuPre. Couldn't you just die?"

"Yeah," I whispered. Tina didn't know the half of it.

I strained to hear what He was saying. It was noisy in the studio, and all I could catch were bits and pieces.

"I'm one of his clients...for one of... Oh. I, uh, that's too bad... No..." Music drowned out the rest for good. He hung up and disappeared into the taping room.

Mickey looked at me curiously.

"You really have the hots for him," he observed dryly.

"So? Let's run through the routine again."

We kept dancing. It's what you're supposed to do, anyway. You wait till after the audition to visit. Even if Mickey had noticed I was acting a little funny over Phillip DuPre, it didn't affect our dancing. The old magic was still there.

In the audition room, the Phillip DuPre behind the table was completely different from the quiet guy who'd shown up at Mrs. Sperling's. There, she was in charge, and He seemed content to let her call the shots. At the audition, this same guy was the boss and knew it, and while He didn't rub it in, He didn't give up one ounce of authority, either.

"Good afternoon," He told us after a friendly smile. "You'll be doing the routine as a group, then as couples. I'm looking for good, precision dancing. I want it sharp, and I want it clean. If you want to show me something, you'll get your chance later."

I had about a second to reflect that Mrs. Sperling was right about Him keeping His biases separate, then we worked. And worked. And worked some more. I was dying when we left the room.

"Geez, that was hard," Tina gasped as we got our outdoor clothes on over our leotards. "I hope I did okay."

"I think I did," said Mickey. He looked at me. "You kicked butt, babe."

"Thanks," I gasped.

"Donna," said Tina. "Earl's working again. Mickey and I were planning on going out to happy hour for dinner after this. You want to come with us?"

"Well..." I hesitated, trying to figure things out. "Mrs. Sperling is expecting me for dinner. But she wants me to run an errand to Emil's later."

"We'll meet you there," said Mickey. "Say, what, nine o'clock?"

"Okay," I said. "Tina?"

"Sure," she said. "Earl will be off by then, too. Come on, Mickey." She hugged me. "You did great."

"You did, too," I answered.

"Later, pard." Mickey reached over and gave me a good sound kiss.

As he left, I turned back into the studio and froze. Phillip DuPre stood in the doorway with one eye on me, talking to one of the men he'd been with. They moved out of the way to let the rest of the people out. Struggling into my jacket, I fled with them.

My beat-up old Altima sat near the studio's doors. Shaking, I unlocked it and got in, then fumbled around the floor to find my keys, which I'd dropped. I finally got them, for all the good it did. The car wouldn't start. Swearing, I popped the hood latch, ran around front, and propped open the hood, which did about as much good as finding my keys.

"Hi."

My heart stopped. Phillip DuPre stood on the sidewalk, looking at me with a half-smile on His gorgeous face.

"Hi," I said, swallowing.

"Car trouble?"

"Yeah." I blushed. "You'd think someone who drives a car for a living would know more about the insides." I slammed the hood shut. "I've gotta call the Triple-A."

"I'll wait with you," he said as I got my mobile phone from my car.

"You don't have to," I said dialing.

"No. It's okay."

"You sure?"

"Yeah," He said as the operator came on.

I gave him the address, he told me it would take up to thirty minutes, and I was to stand next to the car. I hung up with a nervous sigh.

"Something wrong?" He asked.

"Sort of. It's going to be at least thirty minutes

and I've got to wait by the car."

"It's getting dark." He glanced up and down the street.

Cars whooshed past the battered buildings. It wasn't a bad neighborhood, just not a good one for a woman waiting around alone after dark.

"Yeah. I'll be okay."

"I'll wait with you,"

"Oh. Gee." My stomach did three kinds of somersaults and my tongue felt paralyzed. "You don't have to. He said thirty minutes, so you know it's going to be at least an hour."

"I don't mind."

We waited. I called Mrs. Sperling. Then we more or less exchanged nervous grins until the tow truck arrived. I was towed to the nearest repair station. He followed in his car, without being asked. I guess He assumed I'd need a ride, which I did. We exchanged more nervous smiles all the way to Mrs. Sperling's.

He stayed for dinner. Mrs. Sperling had me change, suggesting that I might as well get dressed for my errand that night. We ate in the dining room.

"So, what's wrong with your car?" Mrs. Sperling asked me after we'd said grace.

He'd made the same sloppy sign of the cross that only a true believer makes. Then He stared at his plate as he ate.

"Um, the mechanic said he'd have a full list for me tomorrow afternoon," I sighed. "On the other hand, he said he'd give me five hundred for it."

"For the parts, I presume," said Mrs. Sperling. "Does five hundred sound fair to you, Phillip?"

"Um, yeah. I'd hold out for seven fifty. The worst he can do is say no."

"I still need a car," I said. "I might be able to work out a loan with my parents, or even use the money from this one as a down payment."

"That sounds like an excellent plan, Donna. So, Phillip, have you heard from your supplier yet?"

Everything about Him stopped. He set down His knife and fork, then tried to find someplace to put His hands. For the first time that night, He looked up.

"Aunt Delilah," He said slowly. "I have a confession to make. The reason I didn't tell you the name of my supplier was that I knew he was selling me hot prints. I was trying to win his trust and find out how he was getting them. Then the counterfeits showed up at Josh's place, but they weren't all the same ones, except for some of the Niedemans, so I didn't think Josh's death was connected."

"Only now something has gone wrong," said Mrs. Sperling.

"Big time. I called him this afternoon, and they told me he's dead. They said burglars got him."

"Who are 'they'?"

"His landlady and she said that's what the police said."

Mrs. Sperling nodded. "And your supplier's name?"

"Kyle Hoffman."

"Kyle Hoffman?" I yelped. "He's that building manager."

"Phillip, did you know Mr. Hoffman was the manager of the building where Mr. Stein's gallery was?"

He squirmed. "Yeah, I knew. Why do you think I was suspicious? Besides my Niedemans, Hoffman sold me a couple Gormans, and a Dawna Barton. But Josh didn't even carry them."

"Edgar Hendricks does," I said softly. "Only Hoffman's alibied for Stein's death."

"That does lead to some interesting possibilities," mused Mrs. Sperling. She faded into her thoughts.

The phone rang. I bounced up, but Glen came running in from the kitchen.

"Sorry, I'm late, Mrs. Sperling," he gasped, sliding into his seat at the table. "Donna, it's your brother on the phone."

"Oh, shoot. He probably wants to know about his Niedeman."

"You can assure him it's real," said Mrs. Sperling. "I had it verified. Now, Glen—"

"I'm sorry, but I met this totally bodacious babe. He's, like, a total E-ticket."

My E-ticket smiled His fabulous smile and chuckled.

"Love comes before all. Right, Aunt Delilah?"

I didn't hear what she said. I headed into the kitchen and the phone to do battle with the exact opposite of Phillip DuPre.

"When am I going to get my Niedeman back?"

demanded Peter. "You said it'd be Tuesday at the latest, and it's Wednesday."

"I don't know. My car's broken down, and we're real busy here."

"And I'm supposed to hang while you get around to it?"

"Look, Mrs. Sperling went to a lot of trouble to get that print authenticated for you, and she's not charging you anything, so you could at least be a little nicer."

"Tell her I said thanks. When am I going to get it back?"

"Hang on."

Grumbling, I turned toward the dining room.

"So, Phil, how did your auditions go today?" Glen's voice floated into the kitchen.

I stopped.

"Pretty well," Phillip DuPre said. "Saw a lot of good dancing. I made my point with Slick, finally. The creep begged me to do it because he 'trusts' me, then questioned everything. I told him either pipe down or I walk. But once he saw the dancers, he agreed with me."

"Gonna be a tough choice?"

"Nope."

"Come on. Who're you casting?"

He laughed. "I'm not saying. Got a lot of hassles to get through, Slick's gotta have his say, then the agents."

I went in. "Um, Mrs. Sperling, I've got to figure out how to get my brother's Niedeman to him. He's having kittens."

"Phillip, would you please drive Donna out this evening before you go to Emil's?"

"I thought I was going," I said, surprised.

"But..." He looked puzzled. "Aunt Delilah, you just asked me to go before dinner."

"You're both going," said Mrs. Sperling. "There's already been one incident. I don't want another."

"I told you I wouldn't go alone," I said. "I've got friends meeting me."

"All the better," said Mrs. Sperling. "There's safety in numbers. Donna, where does your brother live?"

"In Pasadena."

"Phillip, that wouldn't put you out, would it?"

"Not at all," He said quickly.

"I don't want to impose," I said.

"If you don't want me to go to Emil's, that's okay," He said.

"Donna, your brother is waiting," said Mrs. Sperling. "Phillip will drive you out to Pasadena, then the two of you together will go to Emil's and meet your friends. End of the discussion."

My heart was breaking. Only the ride out to Pasadena was pretty quiet. I tried to talk but couldn't think of anything to talk about except the auditions, which I didn't want to talk about, and Stein's death, which I didn't want to talk about either. He seemed to be feeling pretty guilty about Hoffman's death, so I decided not to bring that up. He wasn't real talkative.

Peter had plenty to say. Fortunately, Elise

wouldn't let him say it.

"Who's the babe?" she asked me as soon as Peter had Phillip DuPre fully engaged discussing Niedemans.

"A friend of my boss's family," I said, blushing.

He had just introduced Himself as Phil, so I didn't think He wanted me advertising what He did for a living. Peter had given Him the once over and focused on the single diamond earring He wore and the leather bomber jacket. I called it style. Peter probably had other things on his mind, but Elise kept his trap shut for a change.

"Does she have any other friends like him?" asked Elise.

"You're taken."

"You're not. Anything going on?"

"I wish. He won't even talk to me. It's not like he's a jerk. He's really nice, but I can't seem to find anything to say to him."

The guys came back at that point.

"Donna," complained Peter. "You didn't tell us your boss is a private eye. Mom is gonna have fits when she finds out."

I glared at him. "She'll have fits when she finds out you and Elise are living together already."

"You bitch."

"You wouldn't," gasped Elise.

"Peter will just have to see that I don't have to. We've gotta get going."

"Nice meeting you," He said.

"Nice meeting you, Phil," said Peter.

The ride back to Westwood was equally quiet.

I wanted to yell at Him for telling Peter what Mrs. Sperling did with her time. I looked at Phillip DuPre and melted. Hell, how was He to know?

It was just after nine when we arrived at Emil's. It was a bar and restaurant with no dance floor that catered to big business hot shots who worked on Wilshire. Mickey, Tina, and Earl were there. Mickey stood at the bar with a small crowd around him. I could see him working a routine as if he were at a nightclub. Next to him, on the bar, was a glass filled with change and a few bills.

It happened occasionally. Mickey would be entertaining a small group of friends. The group would slowly grow larger as more and more people started listening in. Mickey would set up a glass with some change in it, claiming that he didn't mind going public with his conversations as long as people paid up. He'd gotten thrown out of a few bars that way, but most bartenders didn't care.

"The bouncer comes in." Mickey mugged, instantly turning his body into a Neanderthal. "This guy flunked basketweaving. He says 'Me bouncer, you dead meat.' I said 'But can you shuffle off to Buffalo?'" Mickey did. "He couldn't. I could. I dazzled him with the fancy footwork and lost three teeth. But, hey, it's a learning experience, right?"

The group roared. Mickey went on with his Saturday Morning cartoon routine: Muppet Babies meet the Ninja Turtles. Mickey had seen me and who I walked in with. But Mickey is a professional first and foremost. He didn't miss a beat.

I, on the other hand, was more than a little uncomfortable. I didn't have an ice cube's chance in hell with Phillip DuPre, but I didn't need my ex-boyfriend, who was still in love with me, hanging around at the same time. He'd recognized Mickey, too.

He walked over and put a folded bill into Mickey's glass. Mickey went right on without blinking. I found Tina and Earl sitting in a large booth in the back corner and steered Him that way.

Tina, thank heavens, is too cool to let anyone see her jaw drop. Earl, of course, didn't know Phillip DuPre from Ma Bell, so he didn't care.

"Hi, Donna," Earl said, getting up. "Nice to see you. Who's your friend?"

"I'm Phil," He said casually and shook Earl's hand. He smiled at Tina. "Tina Paulson, right?"

"Yeah." Tina smiled back. She was too cool to talk, however.

"You know Tina?" Earl asked.

"I saw her at the audition today."

"Oh, you're a dancer."

"Not professionally. I do dance."

"Really?" asked Tina.

He nodded. "I studied ballet all through

college. Started too late to do anything with it, though."

"Oh." Tina grinned. "So how did you and Donna hook up?"

"We're not hooked up," I said quickly. "I mean..."

"Uh, Aunt Delilah-" He stammered. "I mean, Donna's boss. She's an old friend of the family. A courtesy aunt."

"She says there's safety in numbers," I said, then smiled weakly at Him. "Not that I mind. I mean, I'm glad you came."

"So am I," He replied quickly.

Mickey called it quits, singing a little theme song that sounded suspiciously like the old "Tonight Show" theme. Grabbing a fresh drink and his glass, he wandered over and squeezed in next to Earl and Tina.

"We must allow august personages some room," he said, mugging.

"I don't see why," Phillip DuPre said, pleasantly. "I was born in May."

Well, that broke the ice, at least as far as Mickey and Tina were concerned. I was still hopeless.

"So, Earl, are you in the business?" He asked.

"No. I'm not that crazy. I'm a resident up at the medical center."

Mickey counted his money. "Crap. Somebody put in a fifty." He looked at Him.

"Not me." He grinned. "I didn't catch the whole act."

"What took you guys so long to get here?"

asked Tina.

"We had to go out to Pasadena," I explained. "My brother wanted his Niedeman back."

"Geez. Introducing Phil to Peter already?" Mickey snorted. He was a little bitter.

"My car broke down, and Mrs. Sperling had him give me a ride."

"That's a hell of a ride."

We all shifted. Mickey sighed. He looked at Him.

"Listen, I don't know what kind of understanding you two got, but can I talk to her for a few minutes?"

"Mickey!" I groaned. "Why don't you just ask me?"

"Okay. Can we?"

Mickey slid out of the booth. I could see him fighting the jealousy. I followed him to the other side of the bar.

He sighed. "Look, I know I haven't got any right to demand an explanation, but I would like to know what the hell is going on."

"My boss introduced us. She's known him since childhood, his, of course. That's all there is to it."

"Oh, really."

"What difference does it make? He and I do not have a relationship."

Mickey groaned. "Donna, get real."

"Okay. I've got a crush on him."

"Just slightly. You sure he's not using you?"

"For what?"

"For what I used you for!"

"Mickey, you never used me."

"Donna, you know I did. And I'd do it again if we ever got back together, and we both know it."

"And you're still jealous."

"Yeah. A lot. But how would you feel if I started hanging with some gorgeous powerful lady?"

"Probably the same." I sighed. "But we're not hanging."

"Then why is he here?"

"We're verifying an alibi. So I happen to be nuts over him. I'm sorry, Mickey. I don't want to hurt you. But I'm not going to live like a nun just because we can't live with each other, and I don't expect you to do the same."

"That'd be a little hard."

"You know what I mean."

"Yeah." He sighed again. "You ever read 'Little Women'?"

"Who hasn't?"

"I feel like Laurie right after Jo turned him down."

"Have you met my sister, Denise?"

"Yeah. She's a nice kid. You got her number?"

"If you call her, don't let my dad know. You got a pen?"

"No. Now what?"

"I'll bum one off the bartender. I've got to ask her some questions anyway."

"Alright. I'll stand guard."

"Did anything happen the last time?"

Mickey shook his head and went back to

the booth. He said something to Phillip DuPre, and they both watched me. I was about to crown Mickey, then thought it was just as well. I looked around the bar to see if Mr. Hendricks was around. He wasn't.

On the other hand, Devon was. Strangely enough, he was surrounded by women at two small tables near the front.

I squeezed onto a vacant barstool. The bartender, a young woman about my age with lots of hair, came up for my order.

"A white wine, please," I said. "And do you have a pen?"

"A singles' joint like this?" Grinning, she handed me one. "You're the twentieth person tonight." She poured my drink with professional ease.

"You usually work Wednesday nights?"

"Every night except Monday and Tuesday."

"How well do you know the regulars?"

"Pretty well. A few of them, very well. Why?"

"Last Wednesday, a friend set me up for a blind date, only I chickened out. We were supposed to meet here, and I think he chickened out also. His name's Edgar Hendricks, and he says he was here all evening, ate dinner, then picked up on a chick and brought her home." I settled in better as the woman next to me left.

"Ed Hendricks?" The bartender laughed. "Since when? Well, maybe once or twice. He's one of those thinks he's so hot types. Most the ladies round here don't need that kind of jerk. They put up with him, but he only scores once in a blue moon."

"Was he here last Wednesday?"

"Let's see. That was the night Harry got sick. No, Ed was definitely not around for that."

"Are you positive?"

"Very. Ed would've gotten sick, too."

"Well, doesn't that beat all." I wrote my sister's phone number on a cocktail napkin. "He did lie. Somehow, I'm glad I chickened out."

"You didn't chicken out." Ed Hendricks appeared from nowhere and grabbed my upper arm. "You're checking up on me."

I stayed cool. "With good reason, it would appear. You weren't here Wednesday night. Where were you?"

"I don't have to tell you."

"But I still know you lied, and my boss will know, too. Why don't you-"

I didn't get to finish. Hendricks backhanded me so hard, I fell off the stool. He was on me in a second, yanking me up, bruising my arms with the force of his grip.

A leather-covered arm dropped around Hendricks' neck in a stranglehold. Hendricks hung on, dragging me along as Phillip DuPre pulled him back.

"Let her go!" He yelled.

Hendricks sent me sprawling backward, then kicked Phillip DuPre in the shins and struggled out of His grasp. He grabbed at Hendricks and missed. Hendricks turned toward Him and tried to run for the door.

People screamed and pulled bar stools out of the way. Phillip DuPre dived. Hendricks got caught and pulled down. Squirming and flailing, Hendricks refused to be pinned. He twisted on his back, swung, and missed. Pulling back, Phillip DuPre lost some of His grip on Hendricks. Hendricks squirmed closer to the door.

Grabbing Hendricks' arms was like trying to catch a windmill. Hendricks' legs whipped about, too, keeping Him straddled over Hendricks' hips, lest the flailing legs put Him out of commission. He flopped down onto Hendricks' left shoulder and immobilized that arm. Hendricks twisted his hips.

The shoe came from nowhere. One second, Hendricks' right hand was empty and the next the dark loafer crashed onto Phillip DuPre's ear. He pulled back in pain. The loafer struck again, landing on His shoulder.

"Yo-yo-yo-yo-yo-yo-yo-yo-yo!" The cry rang out even over the screaming and shouts.

Mickey stood on a nearby table and beat his chest. For a split second, everyone froze.

"To the rescue!" Mickey dove into the fracas.

I scrambled to pull Phillip DuPre back. He scrambled to catch Hendricks. Mickey reached for Hendricks and got Him. Hendricks scrambled between Mickey's legs and got out the door. The three of us fell over each other like the Three Stooges running out after him. Hendricks took off down Broxton, towards Westwood Boulevard. I ran after Hendricks. Mickey ran next to me.

Hendricks crossed the three-way intersection. Tires squealed as cars slammed on their brakes and metal crunched. People were all over. Mickey stopped me at the corner.

"He's gone."

"Dead?"

"No. We lost him. We'll never get through this crowd."

Something was missing. "Where's, uh..?"

"Phil? He's still at Emil's. He couldn't make it. Said for me to go with you."

"He's hurt? Oh no!"

I ran back to Emil's even faster. He sat in a booth near the back. Earl flashed a penlight in His eyes, checking for dilation. Tina held a towel to His ear. A large distinguished looking man in a white shirt, black vest, tie, and pants solemnly watched the proceedings.

"How's your head feel?" Earl asked.

"Okay, except for my ear," He replied.

Earl grinned at me. "Looks like your gladiator is fine. His ear's cut, but the bleeding's slowing down. Probably won't need stitches."

"Oh, no." Sniffing, I flopped down next to Him. "I'm sorry."

"It's alright," Phillip DuPre sighed. "At least you didn't get hurt."

Mickey appeared. "He got away. It was my fault. Sorry."

"I don't care," He said. "Your damned Tarzan act saved my ass."

"It is him," said an average sized man coming up. "Excuse me, Mr. DuPre, I'm Levi Stims, from the L.A. Enterprise."

He groaned and uttered something foul.

"Will you get out of here?" I snapped.

The large distinguished looking man stepped in.

"Mr. Stims, I appreciate your interest, but I must ask you to leave my guest alone."

"And who are you?"

"I own this place."

"But I've got a photographer coming!"

"He will not be allowed to enter."

Mickey slipped away.

"You can't do that," protested Stims. "Freedom of the press."

"This is private property. I am well within my rights to refuse entrance, and to evacuate people when necessary."

Stims took the hint and left.

"We'd better get you out the back," said the owner to Phillip DuPre. "Provided the doctor thinks you can be moved safely."

"Hell with him." He winced as He got up. "I'm moving anyway."

Tina hung onto His ear, as I wedged myself under His arm. I could only hope He wouldn't notice how hard my heart was beating.

"Where did Mickey go?" I asked.

"To get my car," said Earl. "He anticipated our good host's intentions."

For someone in as much pain as He was, He

moved pretty quickly. The kitchen glared after the soft light in the bar. At the back door, Earl looked around, then waved. The sound of his Honda Civic roared up.

Tina, Phillip DuPre, and I squeezed into the back seat. We were barely settled before Earl was in the passenger seat and Mickey peeled out.

"Oh, I love sneaky escapes!" Mickey chortled.

"Sort of makes up for missing out on the fight, does it?" Tina teased.

"Damn you, Phil," Mickey complained good-naturedly. "You get my girl, and you hog the fight. How are we supposed to get along?"

Phillip DuPre laughed weakly. I directed Mickey to the parking lot where His BMW was. Mickey helped us out of the Honda.

"Can you drive?" he asked Him.

"I can," I heard myself say.

"Thank you, guys," He smiled. It was gorgeous. "For everything."

"No sweat." Mickey lightly punched His good arm. "You take good care of her now."

"Mickey, leave!" I yelped, turning purple.

Mickey nodded, then traded places with Earl. I waited until the Honda had disappeared before getting the keys. I helped Phillip DuPre into the passenger seat, then ran around, and slid behind the wheel. He looked at me.

"Um. We'd better got back to Aunt Delilah's. She'll want a report."

"Won't she be asleep?"

"No. She stays up pretty late."

Mrs. Sperling was up. We found her in the living room. The lights were on, although it was some minutes before it dawned on me that they didn't have to be.

"Donna?" Mrs. Sperling asked. "Is someone with you?"

"Yeah."

"It's me," He said. "We had a little problem tonight, and I'm a little sore."

"Oh, dear. Phillip, I really wish you'd take some self-defense training. What happened?"

"Edgar Hendricks caught me checking up on him," I said. "He was really mad that I was, and he wasn't there last Wednesday. I also saw Devon there. You know, the clothes designer?"

"Hm." Mrs. Sperling mused. "Was he also there last Wednesday?"

"I didn't get a chance to check," I sighed.

"Nonetheless, it's been a profitable evening. You'd both best get to bed. Phillip, come on up to the guest bedroom."

ore and stiff, notwithstanding, I went to class the next morning. Back at the house, I showered quickly and dressed even faster. As I left my room, Glen tore down the hall.

"I'm late for class," he gasped and handed me a bundle of envelopes. "Will you give Mrs. S. her mail? And a messenger just delivered that big envelope for Phil DuPre. You know why he was here last night?"

"Uh, yeah."

"He said you could open it since it wasn't going to be here by the time he had to leave." Glen ditched into his room, grabbed books and jacket, and sped back up the hall.

I went into the kitchen. Mrs. Sperling was eating, as usual: veal chops, glazed carrots, broccoli and thin crepes with powdered sugar. I sat down and helped myself.

"Good morning," Mrs. Sperling said.

"Good morning. Morning, Mrs. Osgood."

"Good morning, Donna. I also have carrot bran muffins, if you like."

"They smell like they're fresh, too. Thanks." I took a warm muffin from the basket offered by

Mrs. Osgood and spread butter across the top. It melted, and I had to lick up the little rivulets as they dribbled down the side.

"Did you see Phillip before he left?" Mrs. Sperling asked.

"No. Did you see him?"

"I talked to him briefly." She smiled facetiously.

"Funny," I grumbled, unamused.

Mrs. Sperling frowned. "Were you hurt also last night?"

"I'm a little sore. I'm grouchy 'cause I'm worried about something. There was a reporter from the Enterprise at the bar last night after the trouble broke out. He recognized You-Know-Who. My mother just happens to love the Enterprise and the gossip they post. You-Know-Who told my brother that you're a P.I. last night. My parents are going to be worried sick. If my mom sees that article, if it exists, they won't stop pestering me until I'm back safe in the womb again."

"It can't be helped now. Phillip told me what happened after the man struck you."

"That was Edgar Hendricks. He was lying about Wednesday night, through his teeth. The bartender never saw him, and she seems reliable."

"Given Mr. Hendricks' reaction, I wouldn't doubt her word. Well, that opens up a whole other line of possibility. You set something on the table when you sat down. What was it?"

"Your mail. Glen gave it to me as he ran off."

"Oh, good. Please go through it with me."

I thumbed through the stack. "Mostly bills, it

looks like."

"Those go to my accountant."

"A Braille magazine. You'll have to figure out what it is."

"I'll have to teach you Braille someday."

"A big envelope from D. Froman, postmarked San Francisco."

"A letter from my brother. I'll deal with that. It's probably deathly dull anyway. I'm afraid Dale is the black sheep of our family. He became a banker, married a lovely wife, had two lovely children and went to live in the suburbs."

I snickered. "For shame, for shame. You also have a postcard. From Nepal."

"My parents." She brightened. "Do read it."

"Let's see. What handwriting!"

"That's my father. Everyone complains about it."

"Alrighty. 'Hello, Dolly. Having a smashing time but is it cold in the hills! Had to stop our climb. The guide was afraid your mother wouldn't make it. It's gorgeous here, but Philly says you wouldn't like it. You'd have to keep your gloves on all the time, and you wouldn't see a thing. Tally ho. Off to India. Love, P. and P.'"

"I figured they would while they were in the neighborhood."

"Go to India, you mean? Your folks get around."

"My father has a strong aversion to moss, physical or mental. Fortunately, my mother is blessed with an equal amount of energy."

"Who's Philly?"

"My mother. It's short for Philadelphia. My grandfather was born and raised in that city and put his foot down when the baby was named. Grandma was aghast but too well-bred to argue. My mother comes from a long line of New York society people."

I picked up the envelope addressed to Him. "May as well open this. I was told I could open it. Oh, great. Just what I was looking for."

"A copy of the Los Angeles Enterprise?"

"Right, as always." I thumbed through the first section. "Oh, damn!" I spread the newspaper next to me. "Here it is. Director involved in Westwood bar fight. At approximately eleven o'clock last night, in Emil's bar in Westwood, movie director Phillip DuPre became involved in an altercation with an assailant later identified as Edgar Hendricks, the owner of an art gallery in Beverly Hills. According to witnesses, Hendricks attacked an unidentified female at the bar, when DuPre stepped in and wrestled Hendricks to the floor. Hendricks struck DuPre with a shoe and escaped. DuPre sustained minor injuries and later left Emil's under his own power. Hendricks is believed to be still at large." I looked up. "That's it."

"A small story like that, there's a good possibility your parents will miss it."

"Or they may not realize I was involved. Wait a minute, He didn't tell Peter His last name. My parents will never know."

Mrs. Sperling nodded, then got up and summoned Eleanor.

"Why don't we take the Lexus today," she said as we went out back. "I understand there's a chance of rain, and we have to confront Ms. Bistler again, so we want some authority. I'm also thinking we may want to visit Mr. Hendricks' gallery, too."

"I don't know. After last night."

"I would guess that the newspaper has good reason to believe Mr. Hendricks is indeed still at large. We also must explore the Hoffman matter. It's probably coincidental, but I've a nagging suspicion it's not."

Mrs. Sperling stopped and faded into one of her thinking dazes. I didn't notice at first as I was pulling the Lexus out of the garage. She wasn't paying attention as she loaded Eleanor in the back seat, then got in the front next to me.

"Your seatbelt," I reminded her.

"Oh, yes." She snapped it on. "That's something that simply did not occur to me before, and yet it fits in perfectly with the concept of a conspiracy."

She turned to me, fully conscious. "I just now remembered that all of Glen's other serigraphs are genuine. He got them from Mr. Stein's gallery, which is why he was so surprised when I noticed that his HN4 was a fake. If Phillip's art is all genuine, which I'm fairly certain it is, and he has been getting it from Mr. Hoffman for some time, then there must be a break in Mr. Hoffman's pattern somewhere, which in turn, could lead us to Mr. Stein's murderer."

"Could Hoffman have done it?"

"Then why was he killed? There must be some

sort of conspiracy going on, with the counterfeiting being a new element. Niedemans aren't cheap, but they don't bring in that much money compared to some other things. In a way, it's almost a perfect theft. Who would notice a five-hundred-dollar print missing when you've many other originals for tens of thousands? And if it's worth murder to protect, then there must be other thefts involved, and other people, too. Remember Ms. Bistler's gas purchase? She is a fairly lightweight woman, judging from the pitch of her voice. She couldn't have moved her husband's dead body without some help."

"What if she works out?"

"Unfortunately, she strikes me as being the type of person who is too lazy to exercise beyond what is absolutely necessary to maintain her figure. One doesn't gain that much strength just doing aerobic dance."

"You think she did it?"

"She certainly had motive, and it would appear opportunity. We know she's lying about that night, but I couldn't call that sufficient evidence to convict her. It's too circumstantial. Frequently that's the best you can get. But when it's this sketchy, and I fail to find any more, I look in other directions. I, unlike the police, have the time to do so. It doesn't help more often than not, which is why the police can usually be relied upon to bring the guilty to the courts. Whether or not justice is done is another story and not any of my business beyond that of a concerned citizen."

Neither, really, was her investigation. But I

declined to say so. Mrs. Sperling had a client, and she was entitled to sell her skills at whatever price she wanted, even nothing. She didn't need or want the money anyway.

"Where to first?" I asked.

"Why don't we take care of your car first?"

"I suppose," I grumbled.

At the garage, I held out for seven hundred and fifty dollars and got it in cash. It felt funny cleaning out the Altima.

"I thought I was going to have a party the day I got rid of that turkey," I told Mrs. Sperling as we left.

"Our cars are a part of us, even when unwelcome."

"I just don't know what I'll do for a new one."

"Feel free to use any of my cars, as you see fit. There's no point in them just sitting around most of the time."

"Thanks." I laughed. "I can just see driving myself to McDonald's in the Mercedes."

Mrs. Sperling winced. "The thought of driving to any fast-food emporium in any type of vehicle is not a pleasant one."

"I'll have to take you to Tommy's someday. They have a chili burger people have been known to kill for."

"From what I understand about the neighborhood it's in, that's not at all surprising."

"It's the safest place in L.A. Where to now?"

"Ms. Ramona Bistler's."

"On the double."

Except for a flash of deep teal green from a high-necked silk blouse, Ramona Bistler was encased in a stunning shade of ivory. Her jacket was double-breasted and hip length over a matching straight skirt that stopped several inches above her knees. Her nylons and pointed pumps with ankle straps matched perfectly.

She sat calmly on her couch. Only her chain-smoking gave away her nerves.

"Back again so soon, Delilah?" she asked. "Please sit down. I'm afraid I can't stay long. I've an appointment with my lawyer."

"I doubt we'll be troubling you for more than a few minutes." Mrs. Sperling made herself comfortable on an overstuffed chair next to the couch. "I was just wondering whether you happened to still have the contents of your husband's locker at the health club."

"I never got them. They're still there for all I know."

"Odd. According to the club, you sent a note with a young man to go fetch them."

"I never did that!" Bistler was indignant. "You can't prove I did, either."

"Obviously. That's why I'm here confirming it. It would appear someone has taken advantage of your grief and absconded with your husband's toiletries."

"Why the hell would anyone do that? That's ridiculous!"

"Perhaps not to the person who killed your husband. I suspect there was something in that locker that was damaging. Do you know what was in the locker?"

Bistler thought. "I haven't a clue."

For once, I thought, she was being honest.

"Actually, you do," said Mrs. Sperling. "The same clue I have. Soap, shampoo, conditioner, a blow dryer perhaps, shaving equipment. The normal things one finds in a person's locker, or bathroom. What I'm wondering right now is was there anything else that might be construed as damaging to your husband's killer? Obviously, you don't know. But would you have any idea who might have written that note?"

"Idea?" Bistler stabbed out a half-finished cigarette and lit a new one. "No, I'm afraid not."

"The man was described as young, tall and light-haired. Who do you know fits that description?"

"No one!" she answered quickly.

"You're lying, Ramona. You know at least five men who could fit that description, and you're thinking of someone specific right now."

"Delilah Sperling, I did not allow you into my house to make wild accusations."

"I do not make wild accusations," Mrs. Sperling said. "But I do deduce things and everything about our recent encounters tells me that you have not been entirely honest with me regarding your relationship with your husband."

Bistler suddenly sobbed. "I'm only trying to do what Josh would have wanted me to do."

"So, you were his beard, so to speak," Mrs. Sperling said.

Bistler nodded. "Okay, he was a stick in the mud. And I did marry him for his money. But we did really like each other."

"Why did he feel the need to hide his gender orientation?" Mrs. Sperling asked.

"I don't know," Bistler said. "I really don't. I think it was his family. Maybe it was something about the gallery. I don't know. I didn't really care. I just didn't want to be poor, and Josh totally understood that." She sniffed. "Not having any sex pretty much sucked but I really did like Josh. We had a lot of fun joking about my affairs." She sank into herself. "I'm sorry but I did lie about kicking him out. We really did decide it was time. Both of us. Truth be told, I think Josh was going to come out officially. He didn't say so, but we did agree that it was time for the split. Really."

Mrs. Sperling sat up straight and listened. "What was that?"

"What was what?" Bistler's eyes darted towards the hall to the bedrooms.

"I heard movement."

"Oh that. Um. We're, uh, having a problem with

rats. I've had the exterminators out at least three times this month already. They probably came in with some of the street people we've been having problems with lately." Bistler smiled weakly.

"Yes, that would account for it. One other question, Ms. Bistler. What does the name Kyle Hoffman mean to you?"

As Bistler thought, she calmed down.

"It does sound familiar. Wait. He was at the funeral. I suppose he knew Josh, although it's hard to imagine. Josh was real big on appearances, and Hoffman didn't dress real well."

"How?"

"His suit didn't fit, for one thing. It was tight in the shoulders, baggy at the waist, and the pants were too short, which was really dreadful because he was wearing white socks." She let out a nervous giggle. "Can you imagine wearing white socks with a suit?"

Mrs. Sperling didn't answer. She was in another daze, trying to catch some wisp of a thought.

She sighed. "Lost it." She shook her head. "Well, Ms. Bistler, once again you have been very helpful. Thank you very much."

Once again, Ramona Bistler was only too glad to get rid of us.

As we walked back to the Lexus, Mrs. Sperling stumbled in front of Bistler's Lincoln. She righted herself and continued on. I helped her and Eleanor into her car and drove off.

"Another planned trip?" I asked.

"Trip?"

"In front of Bistler's auto."

Mrs. Sperling cleared her throat. "Yes. It was just as I thought. The engine was still warm, and there is no sun shining. Ms. Bistler has just returned from somewhere. She was not just leaving."

"What made you think that?"

"She had her cigarettes out, and her lighter. I heard her tamping the pack quite frequently as she dug one out. She wasn't tamping a fresh pack as a prelude to putting it in her case. That's a different sound altogether. Nor did I hear her digging through her purse, or fidgeting with it, as she did with nearly everything else within reach."

"She didn't have her purse."

"Which is what I guessed. I believe most women who are about to leave the house keep their purses quite near. But it's not an entirely safe assumption. It could have been she hadn't gotten that far yet. That's why I checked the car. If she had been going out again, I don't think she would have had time to leave it elsewhere and still have her cigarettes in reach. She seems to keep her case with her."

"Like a security blanket. About that rat you heard..."

"It was no rat unless they've taken to wearing rubber-soled shoes."

"He, or maybe she, was down the hall in one of the bedrooms."

"Did you see anything?"

"No. But she looked directly there when you started hearing things."

"You've made a reasonable deduction. The question now is who was back there?"

"Can I make a stab at another deduction?"

"Most certainly."

"Well, given the way she was acting when you called her a liar, how about a tall, young male with light-hair?"

"Brava. Now, who fits that description?"

"Hendricks. Hey. Maybe we're onto something."

"Not so fast. Glen Weir fits that description. Phillip DuPre fits that description."

My heart sank. "Any of a thousand young men in L.A. fit that description. Even Gillian, that clerk from Devonaire, fits that description. Shoot. It looks like we're back where we started from."

"It only looks that way, dear. We're getting closer with each new piece of information. Some of the pieces are even matching up."

"For you, they may be. I'm totally confused. Where do we go now?"

"The Beverly Hills Police station. I need to speak to Sergeant Michaelson regarding the Hoffman murder, and perhaps get some references."

Sergeant Michaelson was in and not at all surprised to find Mrs. Sperling asking about Kyle Hoffman's death.

"It happened around four-thirty. Hollywood says it's pretty easy to tell what happened. Hoffman came home early from work, caught some young punks burglarizing his place, and they beat him to a pulp, probably just for the fun of it. Heaven only knows if we'll ever get it solved. You know as well as I do that's the kind of case that usually ends up in the pending file. Lab went over it real well. Whoever they were, they were smart enough to use gloves. Not a fingerprint there that didn't belong."

"Are they sure about the youths?"

"Yeah. That's the odd thing about it. Officer Willoughby was the one who discovered the body."

"He did? And he's the one you don't care for."

"That's him. He said Hoffman had pulled him over this morning near Stein's gallery and told him he had a hot tip. Willoughby admits he probably should have notified me, but he was hoping to shine a little on his own."

"Looking for a promotion, obviously, and a perfectly natural thing to do. What does he say happened?"

"He went to Hoffman's door, heard suspicious noises inside and entered the apartment. Before he could identify himself, he was attacked by a strong youth with a ski mask on. During the struggle, the youth, and his companion escaped out the back of the apartment, down the fire escape. One of the windows in the bedroom was wide open. The lab boys didn't find anything left behind."

"Hm. Has the autopsy come back yet?"

Michaelson laughed. "Are you kidding? We

lucked out with Stein. The coroner's backed up to their butts this week. Considering what it looks like, they won't put any priority on it. And I can't blame them. They don't have time. Their homicide men are doing the usual routine, bringing in the thugs, questioning the witnesses. The only person the landlady saw was Willoughby. She heard the struggle, but thought Hoffman was moving furniture around until Willoughby appeared and asked her to keep watch so as not to mess up any evidence in Hoffman's apartment. According to Hollywood, she was pretty upset, and not really coherent."

"This is pretty interesting. But somehow I feel confident that this is connected to the Stein murder."

"Based on what? I have to agree with Hollywood. It was a couple of punks, probably doped up and after whatever they could get from Hoffman. It's just coincidence that they happened to pick the guy who was building manager at a place another guy got killed. The Stein murder was a class act, a real sophisticated setup. This thing was brute force, pure and simple, and ugly. We both know more often than not, coincidences are just that."

"You're absolutely right, Sergeant. But I'm not budging from my position this time. Something doesn't feel right about the account. What was missing?"

"Nothing that we can tell. Hoffman's stereo and television were in the middle of the living room floor. Looks like they hadn't gotten far when Hoffman caught them."

"That is the likely conclusion. And the struggle took place where?"

"In a different part of the living room. Near the door. Hoffman was found flat on his back in front of the front window."

"Another likely spot. Something is not right here. It's almost too typical."

"Hollywood sees it regularly. And we see it here too damned often. If you want to worry about it, Mrs. Sperling, fine. You've got the time. I don't. Besides Stein, I've got a dead teenage girl they found off Canon that I still haven't identified. I've got a random shooting incident, and at least eight burglaries, and two robberies, and just to make life interesting three rape cases and a flasher who has taken to showing his wares in the library of all places. Have you ever tried to get an accurate description from a shook-up old society broad?"

"Actually, I have. Sounds like a good place, though, with all those shelves to hide behind. If I get done with this Stein mess before you catch him, perhaps I'll go in as a decoy. He won't be able to show me a thing."

Michaelson had to laugh. "But you won't be able to describe him."

"Height and stature, perhaps, if I hear enough. Have you gotten anything on him?"

"Sketchy. Tall, youngish, light hair, and big where it counts. That's the only thing I can get them to agree on. He sure knows how to pick his victims. We've had a composite in there for a month, and he's struck twice since then. You know what this one lady said? Composites never look like the real person. I asked her what changes we should make to improve this one. She couldn't think of one. Another broad said the only thing she'd recognize was what he was showing, and if she hadn't been so startled, she would have asked him to marry her."

"Sounds gifted," I snickered.

"Donna," chided Mrs. Sperling in a good-natured tone, although I knew she meant it seriously. "I know the situation lends itself to lewd comments, but we needn't make them. Well, Sergeant, I'm afraid I'll have to leave you to your exhibitionist for the moment. Do think of me if you decide you could use a decoy."

"I'll put you on the list. At the top. I've had a lot of volunteers, but I think I'd trust you sooner than most of them."

"Do you know if the Chief is in?"

"He went to some fundraising affair. I'll leave him a message that you need a letter of recommendation for Hollywood."

"That will be most kind of you, Sergeant. Donna, we'd best get going."

"Yes, ma'am. I'm right behind you."

In the car, she directed me to a law office near Stein's gallery.

"Why don't you think Hoffman's death was a coincidence?" I asked before we got there.

"A lot of reasons. One is something Ms. Bistler

said, about Hoffman's socks. I can't think why it's significant, but it seems like it must be. Another reason is that we know Hoffman was selling stolen artwork. The question is, where did he get it? He was doing it often enough that Phillip hoped to gain his confidence, yet why didn't anybody notice any missing? It seems to me a sustained theft like that would have created some stir long before this. Furthermore, Phillip implied that he was not Hoffman's only customer, and somebody was very anxious to dump some Niedemans on Dolores Carmine shortly after Stein's death. That suggests quantity, making it harder to believe that the losses went unnoticed."

"Could Michaelson be covering them up?"

"Not likely. It would be too easy for me to find out, and the sergeant is not that kind of person. He's a very busy man, and he appreciates all the help he can get."

"But you said you didn't like the story itself."

"I don't. It's too perfectly what one would expect to find. And the lab found absolutely nothing. That doesn't make sense. Something almost invariably gets left behind, usually something useless in terms of finding the miscreants, but there is something. Not to mention the fact that these doped up punks were using gloves. Most of their kind are too unintelligent and too intoxicated to remember that. That's the problem, too. These thugs do remember just enough times to make a coincidence probable. No. Sergeant Michaelson is justified in his point of view. But he doesn't have all my information. I shall have to revise my report tonight."

We arrived at the lawyer's office right about then, but it took me several minutes to find a parking place. I finally had to settle for a public lot just off Wilshire and Rodeo. We walked back to the office at a good clip.

That's one thing about Mrs. Sperling. She doesn't dawdle. She says it's because at guide dog school the students are taught to keep up a good pace to keep up with the dogs. But when Eleanor starts looking winded, I say it's because Mrs. Sperling walks fast.

Mr. Stein's lawyer was a younger man, maybe in his mid-thirties, not terribly tall, with light brown hair. He wore a pin-striped suit, but he made it look stylish and trim. His name was Paul Grisom. He greeted us cordially and invited me to sit down with Mrs. Sperling.

"Mr. Grisom," Mrs. Sperling said. "I understand you made out Mr. Joshua Stein's will."

"I handled all of Josh's legal matters."

"We've been given to understand that he left everything to his wife."

"That is correct."

"What is the likelihood of Mr. Stein's relations fighting the will?"

"Minimal, at this point. For one thing, his parents are dead, and he had no siblings. For another, all his other relatives live in New York and are sufficiently well off so that an extended court case at this distance would not be worth it."

"Would they have had much chance at succeeding, especially given that Mr. Stein was estranged from his wife?"

Grisom chuckled. "About an ice cube's chance in hell. Josh revised his will to include Ramona Bistler three days after the separation papers were filed. They might get some mileage out of the sound mind clause, but in the long run, it wouldn't be worth it, especially with the distance factor."

"I see. Ms. Bistler's attorney seemed to think there were fair to middling chances of the will be contested, depending on the family's attitude towards Ms. Bistler."

Grisom laughed full out. "Montoinne'd be thinking that. He's a crafty shyster, alright. He's into Bistler for the bucks, believe you me. I don't think Josh's relatives knew Bistler, and they wouldn't have given a damn, anyway. Based on what Josh told me, of course."

"Does Mr. Montoinne know this?"

"Who knows. I'd have to wait until a court case to find out. Why?"

"He seems to be keeping Ms. Bistler in the dark about a number of things."

"You mean to put the brakes on her fooling around. That's just playing it safe. I would've told her the same thing."

"He also confessed to leading her to believe that her financial status was not as good as it is."

"Of course, he would. Money would be about the only thing that'd keep her out of every pair of pants that came along."

"You don't seem to have too high a regard for Ms. Bistler."

"I didn't like her at all. She was taking Josh for every cent she could get, and he was okay with it. I would drop hints every so often, but Josh didn't give a damn. He liked having a wife, and if she wasn't around that often, fine. I have good reason to believe she was his beard, if you know what I mean. Why he felt he needed to stay in the closet in this day and age, I have no idea. And for whatever reason, he wanted to be sure she'd be well off. Josh was a class A-one lulu, if you ask me. But what am I gonna do about it? I was only supposed to advise him on legal matters."

"Do you know if Ms. Bistler knew the terms of the new will?"

"It's possible. I have no way of knowing. It depends on when was the last time Josh spoke with her."

"Which there is no way of knowing, and no way of asking her without tipping her off."

"I take it you like her for Josh's murder?"

"I don't know at this point, Mr. Grisom. It would appear several people are involved in one way or another. I certainly can't point the finger at anybody with the evidence I have."

"It's a tough one, from what I hear."

"Speaking of that, had you heard any rumors about the gallery?"

"No. It was doing pretty well when Josh revised his will. It's a pity Josh couldn't leave his money to the gallery. He lived and breathed that place. I think it's the only reason he didn't give a damn about his wife being a money hungry slut. She looked nice at the obligatory parties, which Josh hated anyway."

"Hm." Mrs. Sperling mused for a moment. "What about other people Mr. Stein might have had conflicts with? I have heard he wasn't on good terms with a clothing designer named Devon."

"That twit?" Grisom chuckled and shook his head. "If it was Devon that had turned up dead, then I might have had something for you. Josh could not stand him. Apparently, Devon is a spoiled baby, or so goes the local scuttlebutt. Constantly flying off the handle. Given Josh's attitude, I'd believe it."

"That is very interesting." Mrs. Sperling mulled it over, then got up. "Well, Mr. Grisom, you've given me a few more things to think about. I appreciate your time."

"Anytime, Mrs. Sperling." He came around his desk and shook her hand. "I liked Josh, and it really ticked me off to see him being taken advantage of by that bitch. In some ways, I hope she did it and gets what she's had coming to her for a long time."

"Well, vengeance is not my job. Finding the truth is. Thank you, Mr. Grisom. You have been most cordial."

Mrs. Sperling was lost in thought as we walked to the car.

"I have more evidence piling up against Ramona Bistler," she complained as we got in. "And very little of it would hold water in court. There must be a connection somewhere. I keep thinking I've missed it. Oh. It's too aggravating."

"Where do we go in the meantime?"

"Are we in the neighborhood of Mr. Hendricks' gallery?"

"Yes."

"Oh no. I forgot to tell Sergeant Michaelson about him. On second thought, I don't think we have enough against him to justify a search warrant."

"You mean attacking me isn't enough?"

"Not to look at his books. Hoffman had to be getting his prints from someplace. Perhaps Mr. Hendricks can point us in the right direction, seeing as though he had reason to bear a grudge against Mr. Stein."

"We should have walked from the parking lot," I said, as I drove around the block where Hendricks' gallery was located for the third time.

"Hm. It would have been better exercise, too."

"There's one!" I stepped on the accelerator. I hit the brakes as a little red Mercedes cut in front of me and grabbed the spot. "Jackass!"

"It's a good thing we have seat belts."

"Hang on. I just spotted another one, and I'll be darned if I'm going to lose it."

"Banzai," remarked Mrs. Sperling passively. "Is it really worth wrecking the car just for a parking place?"

"No. But the other drivers don't have to know I feel that way. There are some things you just have to bluff your way through." I looked over my shoulder then the dash screen as I backed in. I shifted into drive, pulled forward a little, and checked my position. "I'll be. A perfect two-point landing. I think I'm in love with this car's back up camera."

"I don't doubt it." Mrs. Sperling got out of the car. "On to the gallery."

I was a little surprised to see it open, and nervous. Hendricks was violent and not above dirty tricks. I remembered what Michaelson had said about Hoffman's body and shuddered. Mrs. Sperling did not seem in the least perturbed and walked in without hesitation.

As usual, she knew what she was doing. Another milder man was behind the desk, talking on the phone. He was average size with brown wavy hair. Another woman browsed. The man hung up the phone and approached her, speaking very softly. She smiled and shook her head.

"I'm just looking, thank you."

The man approached us.

"May I help you, ladies?" he almost whispered.

"I believe so," answered Mrs. Sperling. "What is your name?"

"Bob Dorsett." He accented the last syllable.

"Isn't this studio owned by Edgar Hendricks?"

"Yes, but he isn't in today. I'm his associate, and I can handle anything he would have."

"I take it, you often act in his stead."

"I have to. Ed's not always here."

"He was here yesterday."

"Not all day. He left around three thirty. It was something important. He was in a pretty big rush."

"As if he was scared?"

"Ed's always scared."

"He may have good reason this time. Do you know why he isn't here today?"

"He's out of town."

"Was this a planned trip?"

"No. He does that sometimes. Just decides to take off. He called me last night, in the middle of the night, and said he was going, the keys to the gallery were in my mailbox, and they were."

"Did he say where he was going?"

"That's funny. He didn't. He usually does. I wonder if he's in some sort of trouble."

"He is. He's wanted on assault charges by the Los Angeles police. He attacked Miss Brechter, here, last night, and later assaulted her friend when he came to her rescue."

"Oh, geez. Damn that Ed. He has one hell of a short fuse. He knows art, but if you ask me, he isn't all there. He drives people out of here 'cause he thinks he's the only person who knows anything. The only reason this place is still on its feet is because he isn't always here, and because he does know his art." Dorsett sighed. "It's too bad, too. The guy can't run a business worth beans. Never checks up on his back orders, can't get the billing straight. What's a guy like me to do?"

"Make up for his inefficiencies?" Mrs. Sperling smiled.

"Only when he's not here. If Ed thought I didn't think he knew what he was doing, he'd have my head on a plate, and then fire me. That guy has got a temper. You should have seen what he did with this bronze we had. Some customer said it was a piece of... Well, he wasn't very nice about it. Ed got mad. Real mad. Picked up the bronze and heaved into a Niedeman serigraph. Put a dent in the wall, he threw it so hard. The Niedeman was ruined. It was one of the signed ones, too." Dorsett shook his head. "Ed can't afford losses like that. If things don't get better this Christmas, we're going under, and that's a fact. Ed's broke. He won't believe it. He thinks the bank guys that are after him are just out to get him for personal reasons."

"So, he needs money."

"He needs it bad."

Mrs. Sperling nodded. "He wasn't too fond of the Stein gallery, was he?"

"He hated Josh Stein's guts. Josh knew what he was doing, even if he wasn't a big party type. And in Ed's defense, I gotta admit, Josh could be a real stuck-up pain in the ass. But the big thing Ed had against him was that Josh's gallery was doing better than his. Josh couldn't pick his art nearly as well, but he sold a lot more. Ed couldn't stand that."

"Given what I know of his personality, I can imagine he found it a bitter pill to swallow."

"Ma'am, can I tell you a secret?" Dorsett's soft voice sank even lower. I had to really strain just to hear. "Last week, I heard Ed say he had plans for Josh's gallery. He wouldn't say what they were, but he gets this real sneaky grin on his face. The kind I know means trouble. The thing that scares me, the next day they find Josh dead. Somebody knocked him on the noggin and left him in a garage with the motor running. I asked Ed where he was that night. He wouldn't say. He just laughed."

"Interesting. Still, it's not completely conclusive, as I'm sure you're aware, Mr. Dorsett.

Ergo, Mr. Hendricks' continued liberty. Are you aware of the rumors that Mr. Stein was counterfeiting?"

"Those have been circulating for the past year and a half."

"Anything in them?"

"No way. Ed started them, trying to do in Josh's business. Nobody believed them. Josh was too straight. And several people had had their stuff authenticated. It was genuine. Besides, somebody would have to be a real dope to try and sell forgeries out of his own gallery. A bad reputation can kill you in this business."

"Which is precisely why Mr. Hendricks started the rumors, I'm sure." Mrs. Sperling thought for a long moment. "You say the business has been doing poorly. Might I and my associate look at the books?"

Dorsett started. "Why? You're not a cop. You can't be."

"No, I'm a private investigator. Mr. Hendricks may have been the innocent victim of a thief. You made a comment earlier about back orders. If your books reveal what I think they will, it may help explain some things. Would you be so kind?"

"I-I don't know. If Ed finds out, he'll kill me."

"That is, unfortunately, possible. However, I seriously doubt he'll be back today. I won't tell him, and my associate surely will not. That leaves only you to say anything. Can you be trusted to keep quiet about it?"

"How crazy do you think I am? Look, ma'am,

books are something private. You just don't show them to every person that comes through that door."

"I am not every person. Is there by any chance some illegal activity recorded in those books that you do not want me to find?"

"No! No way."

"Then I do not understand your hesitation in allowing me to go over them."

"It's the principle of the thing, ma'am. You're in here trying to find out about Ed. I've already told you more than I should have. But people talk, and in the long run, it's my word against yours, and your associate's. But she's biased for you, so I figure I'm not taking too many chances. The books are written and legal."

"And also destroyable."

"Which would look pretty funny and would get me into all sorts of trouble. Sorry, ma'am, that's too much sticking my neck out."

Mrs. Sperling sighed. "I understand. However, if you don't show them to me now, I shall be forced to have a member of the Beverly Hills police obtain a search warrant for them. Either way, I will know what is in those books. I would appreciate it if I could look at them now, thus saving me a great deal of time, and the taxpayers of this community some money. I might also add, a search warrant would be public, and would certainly arouse Mr. Hendricks."

Dorsett weighed this out. After a minute, he walked over to the desk and pressed a few keys on the computer's keyboard.

"It's all yours," he said with the resignation of a reluctant Christian facing the lions.

Eleanor led Mrs. Sperling over, and I followed. The store's spreadsheet was on the screen.

"Well," I said, scrolling through the page. "It looks like they were making ends meet until July. Before that, they're okay. There seems to be an increasing back-order cost, though, going back, geez, almost a year."

"We've had tons of them," sighed Dorsett. "Mostly last spring. None of the high-ticket items, just prints, you know, serigraphs and lithos. But they added up. Ed wouldn't go after the studios. He told me to wait, and he'd take care of it. But he never did. Ed must have talked to them eventually, 'cause we've been getting full orders since July for the most part. But it was around then that the back orders really began to hurt. Summer's kind of slow for us."

"Who had access to the prints when they came in?"

"No one, except me and Ed."

"Are you sure? There were no other employees at the time?"

"No. It's always just been me and Ed."

"That is awkward. Perhaps if we could look at the packing slips."

"They're in the back-order file with all the others."

I dug them out. It was a thick file. "Okay, here they are. Let me get this paper clip off. The received count is written in red ballpoint ink. The back order is noted in the next column, in black ballpoint ink, and in a different hand than the received. Looks like studio shipping people are not real well educated, which would account for the mistakes."

"It could," agreed Mrs. Sperling. "Well, Mr. Dorsett, I regret that we've caused you any discomfort. But I must thank you for your kindness. This does shed some light on a very intriguing problem. We'll be off, now. Thanks again."

She sighed once we were on the street. I frowned.

"I thought you said we didn't have enough evidence for a search warrant," I said.

"Well, as you said earlier, there are some things you just have to bluff your way through." She shook her head. "It's hard to imagine how people can be so stupid at times."

"Those back orders are Hoffman's hot prints, you think?"

"I'd be fairly positive, except for one thing. How on earth did he get a hold of them?"

"The conspiracy theory again."

"Yes. But who is conspiring with whom? And how does all this fit in with Mr. Stein's murder?"

"Could it have been a personal thing all along, and Hoffman just happened to be mixed up in it?" I looked out at the traffic.

"That would seem rather likely, given Ms. Bistler and Mr. Hendricks. Yet, they are both independent of each other. They both made up separate lies. They both had opportunity, and they both have separate, though powerful motives."

"Where was Bistler when Hoffman was killed?"

"It doesn't matter," Mrs. Sperling said with a shrug. "She didn't know him. You must have noticed how much calmer she became when I asked about him."

"But you said you thought Hoffman was connected to the counterfeiting."

"He probably was. I'm wondering if we aren't dealing with two separate, but related crimes here. The murder could indeed have a personal motive."

"You know. It now strikes me that that Grisom guy had a great deal of venom for Ramona Bistler."

"Does he fit our description?"

I closed my eyes briefly. "Come to think of it, he does a little."

"Which only stops us from eliminating him. But why kill Mr. Stein? It was Ms. Bistler he didn't care for."

"Maybe he had something against Stein that he didn't tell us, like Stein caught him embezzling. Grisom conked Stein on the head, then left him in a garage, waited a while, then returned him to the studio, using Stein's keys. And because he doesn't like Bistler, he tries to push us in her direction. In the meantime, he's fixing the books so if Bistler doesn't get nailed for it, she won't know what happened to the money."

"Perhaps the most plausible scenario that

we've stumbled across. Unfortunately, it's mere speculation without a shred of evidence. We shall have to examine Mr. Grisom more thoroughly." Mrs. Sperling paused as Eleanor held her back from stepping into the street.

"I've got an idea about how to see if he has an alibi for last Wednesday night. I'll pretend I'm a survey taker." I gently tagged Mrs. Sperling's elbow as the pedestrian light turned green.

"He may not answer you. There are those people who do not like being surveyed, and they rarely have anything to hide."

"It's worth a try."

"Yes. But I would recommend waiting until tomorrow at the soonest. He might think it suspicious that someone is so interested in his whereabouts on the night of the murder so soon after we were there. In the meantime, we'd best also look for a connection between Mr. Hoffman and Mr. Hendricks. Wait. It just now occurs to me that the morning we found Mr. Stein, Mr. Hoffman mentioned the rumors surrounding the counterfeits. He must have been in contact with Mr. Hendricks somewhere along the line. But where?"

I shrugged. "Hiding in the back alley? Who knows? I wonder where we look."

"Probably with Mr. Hoffman's associates. They might be less cautious than Mr. Hendricks, or easier to confuse."

"You know, Hendricks was not at the gallery when Hoffman was killed. And that Dorsett guy says Hendricks was prone to violence."

"As you know well from personal experience. That might explain Mr. Hoffman's death, but it doesn't answer the question of Mr. Stein's."

"Two separate crimes. Grisom nailed Stein. Hendricks nailed Hoffman."

"Perhaps. Perhaps. We should still be open to a connection between the two. It could solve the whole puzzle. At the same time, we must not be so concerned with the single crime theory that we unnecessarily obfuscate the matter and thus overlook the solutions to two crimes."

"I stand warned. Where now?" Having reached the car, I clicked the lock open and opened the back passenger door for Eleanor.

"Let us examine Mr. Hoffman's home."

"Will we be able to get in?"

"Not without my letter of reference from Chief Matthews. However, we may be able to gather some information from the outside of the building. And Mrs. Parrish might be able to tell us something."

"Who's she?"

"Mr. Hoffman's landlady." Mrs. Sperling got into the front seat.

"Oh. Right."

It turned out that Mrs. Parish wasn't in when we got there. The building was tan, two storied, with an archway in the middle leading to the apartments built around a courtyard with a pool. It was located off Sunset. The neighborhood was not very well kept up. Bits of paper lay in the gutters and cars sat on the small lawns in front of the apartment buildings. The pool in Hoffman's complex was empty except for a black puddle with yellowed newspaper and a rusty tricycle sticking up out of it.

Mrs. Sperling stayed out on the front walk, while I walked around to the side of the building.

"It's the same tan stucco as the front," I called back to her. "There are two rows of three, four, five windows. One row on top for the second story, and then the first story row pretty much under them. All the first story windows have black wrought iron bars on them. There's maybe six feet between this building and the one next to it." I came back out to the walk. "You know, there isn't any fire escape on that wall. And if Hoffman's apartment is right above the landlady's, it'd have to open out there."

"When you went into the courtyard, did you see a door with a police seal on it?"

"I couldn't tell from the angle I was at. A couple mean looking guys came out of a ground floor apartment, and they were giving me some awful funny looks, so I thought it better to depart."

"A wise decision. This is one area where I do think it best to leave the questioning to the Hollywood division police."

"Still, that fire escape..."

"The sergeant was probably referring to a special window dedicated to that purpose."

"Now I know what you mean. It must have been pretty easy to get down, too, with those buildings so close together."

"Indeed."

A car pulled up behind Mrs. Sperling. It was an older Chevy in bad shape, with peeling dark blue paint and numerous dents. A tired looking Black woman got out, carrying a baby and a sack of groceries. She eyed us cautiously.

"Who are you folks?" she asked.

"I am Mrs. Delilah Sperling. Do you live in this building behind me?"

"I'm the manager."

"Then you are Mrs. Bedeliah Parrish."

"Yes. What you want?"

"Some information regarding the trouble here yesterday."

"You from the insurance?" She almost smiled.

Mrs. Sperling caught the vocal cue. "I understand nothing was actually stolen."

"That don't mean nothing. That damn cop bust my door down. That's why I called you guys. They said it was covered and it's in my policy in black and white."

"I'm sure it is, Mrs. Parrish. Someone will be out soon to appraise the damage. I'm investigating a related matter. Could you tell me in your own words what happened yesterday afternoon?"

"Oh, that's simple. I was coming home from the market when I see that White cop knocking on Hoffman's door. He looked at me, and made the ugliest face, and bust the door in."

"How did you see this when my associate just now tried to get a view of Hoffman's door from the archway there and couldn't see even the police seal?"

"I was coming from the other side where the garages are."

"That would explain it. What did you do when you saw the officer break the door?"

"I didn't see that exactly. I just saw him go in. Later, I know he busted it. I went into my apartment and heard the noise, but I didn't pay it no mind cause Hoffman he was always making noise. Then the White cop, he come down and ask me to keep watch. Says there was burglars in Hoffman's place. I don't mind saying that scared me some, 'specially when the cop says they killed Hoffman."

"You haven't had much trouble here?"

"Honey, we always got trouble. But this was the first time someone got killed in my building."

"Well, thank you very much, Mrs. Parrish. I expect that covers it nicely. You've been most kind."

"Thank you." Mrs. Parrish moved into the building with half an eye on us.

I pulled out of there and headed for home.

Phillip DuPre was waiting for us when we got back to the house. He was dressed up in a dark, shimmery jacket with a dark purple shirt, tie in gold, olive green and purple, and black dress slacks.

"Splice-Man's got her covered," He told Mrs. Sperling. "Iggy and Bernie are waiting elsewhere. I figured I'd better take restaurant detail, just in case she goes someplace where we'll need some influence to get a last-minute reservation."

"Excellent, Phillip." Mrs. Sperling smiled. "Donna, why don't you get dressed and accompany Phillip? I'm sure he won't want to eat dinner alone."

Not to mention how much I wouldn't mind being his guest.

"Won't you need me?" I asked anyway.

"Not tonight. I'm staying in."

"Well, I do have that money from my car."

"My treat," He said quickly.

"Oh. You don't have to."

"No problem."

"Hurry, Donna."

I dressed in record time. They were in the

living room when I finished.

"I'm ready," I announced a lot more casually than I felt.

"Well, Phillip," said Mrs. Sperling. If I hadn't known her better, I would have sworn she was smirking. "How does Donna look?"

His eyes went up and down my yellow polished cotton shirtwaist with the full skirt. I was wearing black patent sling back pumps and black chunky jewelry, too. I'd also left the bottom two buttons on the skirt undone. My legs are my best asset, and so what if nothing was going to happen. I had a black lacy cardigan in my hand in case it got cool.

"Nice," He said softly.

"Good. Now where were we?" Mrs. Sperling thought. "Ah. We talked with her attorney. He'd told her to avoid romantic liaisons until the will was settled. He seemed to be afraid it might be contested."

"Montoinne would," He said with a chuckle.

"You know him."

"Sort of. He's a funny old bird. Was basically straight and sober until his wife died a couple years ago. Then he went into a mid-life crisis for the books. Started hanging around some pretty interesting females, including Ramona."

"He did indicate that their relationship was more than professional. However, strangely enough, Paul Grisom, Mr. Stein's lawyer, said there was only a minimal chance that the will would be contested. I wonder if Montoinne knows that?"

He shrugged. "He could. He's got pretty good hearing, if you know what I mean."

"Then why would he be interested in restraining Ms. Bistler, so to speak? And why would he be concerned, when he knows Ms. Bistler doesn't need Mr. Stein's money to be comfortable? Although, I might add, Ms. Bistler doesn't know it."

He laughed. "It's perfectly simple. Montoinne's jealous."

"Jealous? Of what?"

"Of dear Ramona's many other boyfriends. Mid-life crisis or not, Montoinne's still a stuffy old bird at heart, and believes in one man per woman, even if she has to share. A sexist attitude, admittedly, but not surprising from one of his generation."

"Not in the least." Mrs. Sperling shook her head. "How do you know so much about him?"

"I've seen him at parties, things like that. And I hear things, too."

"And how do you know what's malicious gossip and what isn't?"

"That's just it. I don't. But I heard them fighting a few weeks back. I didn't catch much, but more than enough to know what it was about."

"Hm." Mrs. Sperling mused.

"Um, might I ask what we should be looking for?" He looked at her hopefully.

"Anything and everything, of course," Mrs. Sperling replied blithely.

"What are we doing?" I asked.

Mrs. Sperling smiled again, that almost smirk.

"You are going to be, as it is known in the jargon, tailing Ms. Ramona Bistler."

"Why?" I asked.

"To see what happens."

"Oh. We'd better get going."

Mrs. Sperling shook her head. "Not yet. Phillip's friend, Mr. Davies, hasn't telephoned us with Ms. Bistler's whereabouts."

"What if she stays home?"

"I had Glen call and ask if a mutual acquaintance might drop by this evening, and she insisted she would be out."

A cellular phone tweetered. He picked it up.

"Yo, Splice-Man." He listened. "No kidding.... If I can't, I'll have Iggy get some chow for us.... Uh, yeah, Aunt Delilah's new driver.... Don't ask me.... Never mind. You meet up with Iggy, and we'll call with the next location.... Yeah, bye." He flashed a weak grin at me, then turned to Mrs. Sperling. "She went to Mr. G.'s."

"Oh, dear. Will you be able to get a reservation?"

He shrugged. "It's Thursday night, and they're really Industry conscious."

He looked up the number on his iPhone and dialed. He looked at me, and I swear, blushed as He made the reservation for twenty minutes later. He looked over at Mrs. Sperling.

"Geez, it's so embarrassing when I have to play Industry heavyweight," He told her.

"Well, darling, be thankful you are, and I'll be thankful you don't have the ego to go with it. Run along, now, both of you, and be careful."

It was another quiet ride over to the restaurant that was currently "the place to be." It was so hot, even People magazine hadn't caught onto it yet. I tried to be blasé about it. It was filled with "names." Several came over to say hello. He was cool, and greeted them politely, and introduced me as a friend of a friend.

One producer, I forget his name, made some inane comment about blind dates. I thought I would sink through the floor. My sort of date just laughed and said even blind dates sometimes worked out.

Ramona Bistler was there but didn't see us. She was with another woman.

"You wouldn't happen to know the woman she's with?" I finally asked Him as we ate.

He looked over my shoulder, then back at his plate.

"Rita Cartlin. She's married to Niles Cartlin."

I grimaced. "I should know that name, shouldn't I?"

He shrugged. "He produces a few sitcoms. Not a bad name to know, but not a real heavy hitter, either."

"Oh." There was silence. "What do you know about his wife?"

"Rita?" He chewed thoughtfully, then fidgeted with his fork. "I've heard she's no stranger to other men's beds. There's another rumor floating around that she slept with some nameless network mucky-muck to get her husband's first series on the schedule. His ratings are respectable, so it may or may not be true. She and Ramona seem to be soul mates."

He looked over at Bistler and Cartlin speculatively, then looked at me and went back to His plate. He paid as soon as He ordered dessert.

"Got to be ready to move," He explained.

"Right." I, too, concentrated on eating. I couldn't think of anything to say.

I figured He thought I was a total idiot. He only had me with Him to please Mrs. Sperling. I must have been boring Him silly.

He started. "They're leaving."

He ducked His head as they went past, then looked at me. I gave them half a second's lead.

"They're almost to the door," I whispered.

"Good. Let's go."

We ambled out. He pretended He didn't hear some big shot saying hi. Cartlin was getting into a limo, while Bistler waited for the valet to bring her car. We were self-parked on the street. We slid out behind her, and got into His BMW, just as Bistler got into a bright red Ferrari.

"That'll be easy to follow," He said, then smiled.

We followed her to Westwood. She had her car valet parked off Westwood Blvd. and went into a bar there. He parked near there and grabbed the phone.

"Hey, Bernie, she's at The White Elephant.... Okay, we'll park it, and next stop, we'll all rendezvous...." He wrote down a phone number. "I've got it.... See ya."

He hung up.

"Wh-whose number?" I asked.

"Splice-Man's new phone. I've already got Bernie and Iggy's numbers."

"Oh."

"They're friends of mine from film school."

"Oh."

I tried to figure out who they could be. Given Phillip DuPre's status, they had to be some kind of hot shots. I didn't want to embarrass myself by asking who they were.

Meeting them didn't help. We rendezvoused in Santa Monica, at another fancy hot spot. Splice-Man turned out to be Edouard Davies, a short black man wearing black 501s and a red double-breasted western shirt. Iggy, or Ignatius McMartin, was taller, quiet, with curly brown hair and glasses. He held onto Bernie, who was really Bernadette Bernstein. She wore a bulky sweater over dark, slim pants, and was a buxom lass indeed.

I was introduced as a dancer, moonlighting as Mrs. Sperling's chauffeur and aide-de-camp. That's when Bernie decided she did not like me. It was more of a mama-bear type reaction. She and Iggy were obviously very tight.

I hung back and let them talk. From the conversation, I guessed that Splice-Man and Iggy were both film editors, and Bernie was a sound engineer. Bernie and Iggy were finally getting married because Bernie was pregnant. During the cheering, I noticed Him looking at me. For no reason at all, I went purple, and gazed about the bar.

Bistler was busy dancing with anybody and everybody. She didn't seem to know the guys, or even care. A tall, blonde figure that could have been a man or a woman, glared from the bar.

"Gillian," I said suddenly.

"Who?" He asked.

"Gillian. They work for Devon, from Devonaire. They're standing at the bar."

Bernie shrugged. "Devonaire. That's that boutique down on Melrose. The clothes are nice, but too pricey for me. That Devon sure is weird, though."

Phillip DuPre laughed. "I've met him before."

I pointed to the dance floor. "And he's here, dancing."

"So, Phil," teased Splice-Man. "You've got a dancer with you. Why don't you ask her to dance?"

He looked at me and got up. "Sure. If you want."

"I guess."

Not only was He gorgeous, He could really dance. I was in heaven. All I lacked was something to say to Him. Bistler left, and Splice-Man slipped out after her. He kept me dancing. The D.J. called a break. As we went back to our table, Devon took off. I hurried after, but by the time I hit the street, he was gone.

I went around the table to the restroom, sulked for a minute, then went back to see if Gillian was still around. They weren't.

With the music off, the rumble of voices filled the room. Bernie and Iggy were facing me, and He had His back to me as I came up to the table.

"I don't know," He was complaining. "I just don't think Donna likes me."

"I don't like you?" I heard myself screech. "Where'd you get that crazy idea?"

He whirled and turned red. "But... But... You won't talk to me."

"Well, you won't say anything to me." Utterly frustrated, and embarrassed to death, I flopped into my chair. "Besides, what do you say to your favorite god?"

"Who? Phil?" asked Bernie.

"Shut up, Bernie," he said. He turned back to me. "Am I that intimidating?"

I grew hotter, if that were possible. "I don't know. I've never known any big names before, and I can't imagine you being interested in a peon like me."

The phone had to ring then. We took off to meet Splice-Man in Century City.

"I'm sorry," I told him. "I didn't mean to embarrass you in front of your friends."

"You didn't embarrass me."

"I said some pretty stupid things."

"What? Like I haven't?" He checked his blind spot, then whipped into the next lane.

"You must think I'm an idiot."

"I don't think you're an idiot."

"But—"

"Will you please be quiet for a few minutes?

I've got to think this out."

Like I was going to say anything more? My head filled with visions of my career going down the drain, all because I opened my fat trap one time too many. I was certain he hated me and would see to it that I never worked in Hollywood again.

"Alright," he said as we pulled onto the Avenue of the Stars. "You like me. That's fine. You're too intimidated to say anything. I can understand that. Sort of. Hasn't Aunt Delilah said I'm okay?"

"Yeah," I sighed.

"Then what gives?"

I glanced at him nervously. He smiled gently. Oh well, He could only black list me once.

"I remember the first time I saw you, I joked with my friend, Tina, that I would love a chance to fall in love with you. Then Mrs. Sperling brought me to your door, and I went under. I was floored. It's not just the name. You're so good looking, and nice, except you didn't say anything to me. Not that I was that brilliant."

His hand softly took mine. "I remember White Heat. I loved your dancing, but I needed lusty, which is why I hired a girl with tits. When you turned up on my doorstep, I about died. You were even cuter then." He pulled his hand away so he could get the car parked. "I guess I'm just like everyone else in Hollywood, completely neurotic and no self-esteem. I get around a woman I like, and I'm completely tongue-tied. I go back to being that nerdy fourteen-year-old whose only experience with women was reading Playboys stolen from my best friend's father." He looked at me again, a bemused smile lighting up his face. "You like me."

He opened the door.

"Um," I said.

He grinned. "Yeah. I like you. A lot."

Two and a half hours and three bars later, Phil and I were finally calling each other by name, although as far as conversation was concerned, we seemed to be repeating Sally Field's Oscar speech a lot. Ramona Bistler went home. By herself.

"What a washout," I grumbled as Phil parked the BMW across the street and down a little, where it wouldn't be obvious but there was still a good view.

"Tonight has not been a total loss," he chuckled.

"No. Why are we stopping here?"

"To watch the house."

"Are we going to stay here all night?"

"I doubt it." Phil yawned. He had sent his friends on home. He stretched, then let his arm fall across my shoulders.

"So why are we watching?"

"I'm not sure. Maybe she'll leave again."

"Maybe." It wasn't that late, and I couldn't complain about where I was. "She didn't do a darn thing, and the only person she saw that could be connected to anything was Devon."

"And Aunt Delilah didn't seem terribly worried about our physical safety." Phil mused. "However, she did seem very anxious that I take you with me, personally."

I looked at him. "She wouldn't."

"I think she did. She knew how crazy I am about you. I spent enough time telling her."

"I did my fair share of sighing about it, too. So that's why she insisted you drive me out to Pasadena. That sneak."

"I can't complain."

He moved in. I went to meet him.

"What's that?" I yelped, pulling back at the last second.

A lone figure ran across Bistler's lawn.

"I'll go find out," said Phil.

"No!" I held him back. "That place has got to have at least thirty alarms hooked up to the police."

"We were necking when we saw this suspicious character and decided to see if we could get a better look at him. Aunt Delilah will back us up. Besides, why would I want to break into Ramona Bistler's house? Or anybody else's, for that matter? Why don't you call the cops? I'll be right back."

Nervously, I picked up my phone and dialed. It took about three minutes to get through everything. It might have taken less time, but I got tongue-tied when I told the operator my friend was trying to get a better look at the intruder, and she asked for his name. She didn't notice a thing. I even had to spell it for her.

Phil had yet to show up. I got worried and left the car. A tall, spare figure came around the corner of the house. Lamplight glinted on his light hair. He didn't look quite right. I figured it was the dark.

"Phil!" I called softly.

The figure ran back where he'd come from. I chased after him. Just as I got to the corner of the house, I was grabbed. I screamed. A hand clamped over my mouth, cutting it short.

"You idiot!" Phil growled. "What do you think you're doing?"

"He went that-a way!" I pointed.

"Can't be. He's breaking into the garage."

"Tall and light-haired?"

"No. Short and dark, with a moustache."

"Lansky?"

"The chauffeur. Right. What does he want here?"

"And who was that other guy? To hell with Lansky."

I started around the corner, but Phil held me back again.

"It's too dark and overgrown there," he hissed. "We'll go around the other way."

"But what if he comes around this way?"

"Alright. You stay in front."

I followed Phil to the other edge of the house. Phil made me wait at the corner.

"Sexist," I grumbled.

A minute later I heard several thuds, shoes

scraping across stucco, and a couple ominous oophs. I started back but was pushed aside by a running figure. I ran after. I hadn't grown up playing football for nothing. I tackled the man at the end of the driveway.

I made one fatal error. Once I had him down, I had no idea what to do with him. He heaved up. I fought for my grasp and hung on. He rolled over on top of me. I gasped as he sat up on my midsection. He swore as he saw my legs. He knew I wasn't very heavy, but I guess didn't expect to find I was a woman. I pounded on his back. He jumped to his feet and was blinded by a bright white light.

"Police! Freeze!"

I was so glad when he didn't make a run for it. I waited until the officers had Lansky in their grasp before stirring. It startled the hell out of one young man about my age.

"You alright, lady?" he asked, as I got up.

"Yeah. Fine. Oh no! My friend!" I ran to the side of the house.

Phil slowly made his way out.

"Are you alright?" I asked and slid under his arm.

"Oh. I'm okay. Where's that damn Irishman when I need him?"

"Irishman?"

"You know. Your friend."

"Mickey. He's only half Irish. The other half's Swedish."

"No kidding. I'm half Swedish. On my mother's side."

The young officer came up. "It looks like we got him."

Another patrol car pulled up, and two more officers fell out and prowled around the grounds.

"There's a second one," I said. "I think he went into the house."

A female voice shrilled out, cursing in all manner of foul language.

"Hey!" an officer called from the back. "There's a forced window back here. Goes into a bedroom."

An infuriated Ramona Bistler appeared in a skimpy negligee from her front door.

"I demand to know what is going on here!" she shrieked.

"Lady, someone has been trying to break into your house," said a big burly officer with a red moustache. "We think there may be another one still in there. You just stay put until we say it's clear. Alf, get the broad a blanket."

Bistler shivered. Well, it was cold, and she wasn't wearing that much. The young officer presented her with a grey woolly affair. Bistler snatched it and wrapped it around herself.

"Ramona!" said Phil, in feigned surprise. "Is this your house?"

She cursed again. "Phil, what the hell are you doing here?"

"We had just stopped to neck when we saw someone running across your lawn."

"Neck? With who?" Bistler stopped when she saw me. "Her? I thought she was driving Delilah Sperling around. When did she start driving you?"

"I just drive him nuts," I said with a little grin.

Bistler was too nervous to notice. She kept looking at the house. A few minutes later, the officers said it was all clear, but they wanted to have a lab team and detectives look at the forced window.

Bistler sighed with relief. Phil and I followed her inside as if we belonged there. Officers went back and forth between the front door and Bistler's bedroom. I walked back and peeked in. By that time, the detectives had arrived with the lab truck. One man dusted for fingerprints, while another photographed the outside.

I walked all the way into the room. The bed was a mess, with one set of pillows on it, pushed to the left. On the right-hand nightstand was a small brass lamp, pushed to the back of the table. Its shade had been knocked askew. Under the lamp were two dimes. On the floor, next to the stand, a brass card case lay up-ended in a V-shape. Several white business cards were scattered under the case, and three pennies and a nickel lay close by.

I bent down to look at the cards.

"Officer," I asked. "May I have one of these?"

He came over and looked at the nightstand. "So, her lover took off. Go ahead."

I slid the card out carefully. Even if the officer was more interested in people getting in, I was interested in the man who had gotten out. I read the name on the card and smiled.

Phil and I called Mrs. Sperling from his iPhone. It was only twelve fifteen, and she was still up. We went by the house and brought her and Eleanor to the police station. She had called Sergeant Michaelson, and he was there waiting for us, yawning, and wearing a beat-up velour sweat top and jeans with a bagging seat.

"You think this Lansky guy's important?" Michaelson asked as we walked in.

"I won't know until you question him, Sergeant," Mrs. Sperling said. "I regret getting you out of bed on mere speculation, but as I explained on the phone earlier this evening, it is a very ticklish situation, and best resolved as soon as possible."

Phil looked at me, and I shrugged. I had missed that call. Michaelson yawned, and led us down to the questioning rooms. He looked at the detective standing at the door. In a most eloquent shrug, the detective said odds were fifty-fifty that Lansky would talk.

Mrs. Sperling went into the room with Michaelson. Phil and I watched through the one-way glass with another cop. Lansky sat huddled in a chair.

"Okay, Lansky," said Sergeant Michaelson. "We've got you on breaking and entering charges. What have you got to say for yourself?"

No answer.

"Mr. Lansky," said Mrs. Sperling. "I would recommend your full cooperation. Without it, the charges could be as serious murder one."

"She's not fooling, Lansky." Michaelson added the official voice.

"Murder!" Lansky squeaked. "I haven't done nothing like that. Honest."

"What were you breaking into your former boss's house for?" asked Michaelson.

"To get some stuff. It belonged to me. I needed it."

"Then why didn't you just ask her?"

"It's perfectly understandable why not, Sergeant," broke in Mrs. Sperling. "Even if Ms. Bistler did not disapprove of her former chauffeur's drug use, she might have asked for her share of his stash, or even taken some without asking. Unfortunately, being unemployed put Mr. Lansky in a definite bind, as cocaine remains a very expensive habit to maintain. Isn't that it, Mr. Lansky?"

"How'd you find out?" he snarled. "I said nothing about it to your driver. Or did you already know?"

"I knew nothing about it until just now. It was mere guesswork, Mr. Lansky. Why wouldn't you have wanted to have Ms. Bistler fetch your possession, something you didn't want to admit to the police was yours, unless it was contraband? You had also expressed a rather suspicious, though perhaps deserved, paranoia regarding me in that encounter with my chauffeur which you mentioned just now. It was also something you needed desperately enough to risk an electronic security system and the presence of people in the house. Given the symptoms of cocaine use, its addictive nature, and it's prevalence, it was a fairly safe guess."

Lansky backed down. "All right. She kicked me out so fast, I couldn't get everything together. It was in the garage. I figured I'd wait a few days to let it die down, then go after it. I had to get it. These guys are into me for five hundred bucks. They wanted their shit, or they wanted their money and fast. What am I s'posed to do? Look, I'll give you their names. Pitch Corsky and Dick Rider. If they killed somebody, I don't know nothing about it, honest!"

"Do you know Kyle Hoffman?" asked Michaelson.

"Who the hell's he?"

"One other question, Mr. Lansky," Mrs. Sperling asked. "On what kind of terms were you with Ms. Bistler's late husband?"

"Oh, it's that murder." Lansky swore. "I got friends can vouch for me that night."

"Answer the question, Lansky," growled Michaelson.

"Mr. Stein? I don't know. He drove himself most times. In the Ferrari. I hardly ever talked to him."

"What do you know about rumors that he was counterfeiting?" asked Mrs. Sperling.

"Oh, hell, everybody knew that. I never seen him do it. But lots of people said so."

"Who were they?"

"People. I don't know. You go to parties, the maids bring back the noise to the drivers. You know how it goes."

"I'm afraid I do." Mrs. Sperling sighed. "I strongly suspect that's the best we're going to do, Sergeant. Nebulous rumors at parties are all too common, and impossible to trace. Besides, I already have a source for the rumors. I was hoping to find a connection." She got up. "I've asked all the questions I needed answered."

"I got no more, either." Michaelson yawned. They left the room. "Damn it, Mrs. Sperling, that was a big fat zero."

"On the contrary, it was extremely productive. We can now eliminate Mr. Lansky, and at this stage in the game, that is a major help."

Officer Willoughby appeared from another questioning room.

"Evening, Sergeant," he said, grinning. "Just brought a suspect in on the Morris burglary. Grant says he wants to question her. Oh, hello, Mrs. Sperling."

"Good evening, Officer," Mrs. Sperling smiled pleasantly.

"Evening, Willoughby," Michaelson growled. He did not look happy.

"Well, I've got to get back to my beat," said Willoughby, and left.

Michaelson yawned again and nodded. He went his way, and we went ours.

"Was the capture of Mr. Lansky the total profit of your evening?" Mrs. Sperling asked Phil and me as we walked through the halls.

"Not quite," I said. "I hit the jackpot. Get a load out of what I found in Bistler's bedroom." I gave her the business card. "It's engraved. Can you read it?"

"It's not a good typeset for my kind of reading, but..." She smiled. "This is most interesting. What do you suppose Mr. Hendricks was doing there?"

Phil burst into loud laughter. I shushed him, then told Mrs. Sperling about the bed and nightstand.

She nodded. "An excellent piece of deduction."

"Not necessarily. The detective took one look at the scene and guessed the same thing."

"All you need is the practice."

"Oh, and we also saw Devon and Gillian at one of the places Bistler went." I sighed. "I lost them, unfortunately, and we didn't see hide nor hair of them after that."

"Did either of them talk to Ms. Bistler?"

I shook my head. "Not that I saw."

"Me, either," said Phil.

"Still, you're right. It is interesting that their paths crossed. How was your evening otherwise?"

"Bistler was a bore," Phil answered. "Granted she did have someone at home waiting for her. But you knew that, didn't you, Aunt Delilah?"

"What?"

"Your little matchmaking scheme. We know when we've been set up." Phil gave me a little squeeze. "And we're pretty glad."

"Well, I'm glad things are working out so nicely for you. But matchmaking? Good heavens, Phillip. I wouldn't dream of meddling in that way. It can have the most deleterious effects."

Phil wasn't listening, nor was I. Our eyes caught, and while it was not the most romantic moment, it was the right one. We kissed.

Mrs. Sperling paused. "Phillip? Donna?"

We ignored her.

"Oh, for heaven's sakes. Granted we are in a police station, and it is the middle of the night. But when you two are with me, I would appreciate it if you would maintain a modicum of decorum."

Phil grinned, and brushed my nose with his finger.

"Just a modicum," he said.

17

The tension was almost unbearable. Phil was meeting that day to cast the video, and I had no idea whether or not I had the job, or given our entanglement, whether I wanted it. Brooding wouldn't help so I stomped into my bedroom and grabbed my tap shoes. On an impulse, I also grabbed a framed Harvey Edwards print I'd been thinking of hanging in my room.

I stomped into the T.V. room and tossed my shoes next to Glen's stereo. The walls were covered with his art, mostly pictures of women, and two of his precious Niedemans. I took one down and replaced it with my Harvey Edwards.

It was a fair-sized room, with a wood floor, partially covered by an oriental rug. Along one wall was a series of bookshelves, and two windows. Pillows were scattered about, and there was a big pile in front of the T.V. located in a corner next to the bookshelves. Glen's super system stereo, complete with digital turntable, radio, boosters, streaming computer and two four-foot-high speakers took up a good portion of the wall opposite the windows. Mirrored tiles had been stuck onto the adjoining wall in patches. A small stack lay on the floor next to it.

Glen had been taking down the tiles because he didn't like them. I decided I was going to put them back up. I went over and stuck one in a hole. It stuck for about three seconds, then came tumbling out. I just barely caught it.

I sighed. I was going to have to get some glue. I'd ask my father. Dad knows all about all sorts of stuff like that.

I stomped over to the stereo, and got my phone connected. It took me a minute to find the song I wanted. While I was trying, I vented on the poor phone. I finally found the song, put it on pause, and put on my tap shoes.

I warmed up quickly. I wasn't stressed enough to risk a pulled muscle. I rolled up the carpet, and slammed on the music. The beginning was slow, so I warmed up my ankles with toe taps.

I was ready when the main body of the song started. Facing the mirrors, I went into the relaxed time step. It was a routine I'd learned years and years before. I liked it because it had lots of stomping in it.

About a third of the way through the song, Glen appeared.

"Why are you dancing?" he asked.

"I'm tense about the video."

"You're going to ruin the floor with those."

"I don't care right now." I made a mental note to get some masonite pieces to cover the floor when I was tap dancing. I paused for the section where the heavy stomping came in, accompanied by lots of fast shuffles.

Glen watched. Usually anything that isn't completely modern doesn't interest him. But I think he was impressed. He waited until the song was over. Breathing heavily, I turned the phone off.

"What was that?" Glen asked.

"'Anything Goes' by a genius named Cole Porter. It's from the show by the same name."

"I think I've heard of it. Where's Mrs. S?"

"At the Braille Institute until one thirty. She's giving Delsie Simmons an extended session."

"Poor Delsie." Glen started picking at one of the tiles.

"Don't you touch those!" I snapped.

"I've been trying to get them down since I got here."

"They're going back up. I live here, too, and I reserve the right to put my influence in also."

"But they're awful. The person who put them up had no taste. You should have seen my room before I moved in."

"Those tiles are practical. With this nice wood floor, and no furniture, I can practice my dancing. That's why I need the mirror. We can make this room a little studio, and roll out the rug when we want to watch T.V."

"That rug is going, too."

"That rug is an antique and worth money."

"Who'd want it? It's ugly."

"It's a nice-looking rug."

Glen grimaced. "No, it isn't. I was going to do

this room up with director's chairs to match the floor..."

"No chairs, unless we can fold them up. I need floor space."

"But it's totally ugly."

"I happen to like it."

"You have no taste." Glen grinned with lofty airiness.

"I have excellent taste."

"Not unless it's mine."

"Who are you, the arbiter of all taste?"

"Yes."

I rolled my eyes, and sat down, stretching out.

"Well, Mr. Arbiter, keep in mind, you're not the only one who lives here. If those tiles come down, and this room gets cluttered with furniture, there's going to be hell to pay."

"What are you going to do?"

I just grinned at him. Glen swallowed. I laughed.

He shrugged. "You mean do the room like a dance studio? Yeah, we could do that. It'd look totally rad."

I took off my tap shoes. "I'd better get going. Mrs. Sperling sent me home to make a whole pile of phone calls."

"Anything more on the murder?"

"I'm almost positive it was Bistler and Hendricks working together. We've just got to get the evidence."

"How about my Niedeman?"

"I know somebody who's selling them cheap."

"Who?"

"Dolores Carmine."

Glen's face fell. "She's out."

"Speaking of her, Mrs. S. wants you to stick around today. She's got a job for you."

Glen shrugged. I went to make my calls.

The first was to the company that had employed Kyle Hoffman. I got handed around three times before I was able to ask my questions.

"This is Miss Browning," I told Mr. Haggerty from personnel. "I'm calling to verify a credit application one of your employees made to us. His name is Kyle Hoffman."

"Hoffman? He died two days ago."

"Oh. Well, just so I can get the record straight, he was employed by your company to manage a building at this address." I gave him the address of Stein's gallery. "Is this right?"

"Yes. He's been with us since July of this year."

"You wouldn't have his former place of employment, would you?"

"Let me pull up the file." There was about a minute's pause while Mr. Haggerty clicked the keys on his computer. He gave me the address, and the exact date of Hoffman's departure from his former job and his date of hire there, which I wrote down.

"Thank you, Mr. Haggerty."

"Um, Miss Browning, pardon me for asking, but your company isn't going to make a loan to a dead man, is it?"

"I doubt it, Mr. Haggerty. It'd be very hard for

him to pay it back. Thanks again." I hung up fast.

I compared the address I'd written to Hendrick's business card and smiled. My next call went through right away.

"Mr. Grisom, my name is Elizabeth Barrett, and I'm with Entertainment Plus. We're a marketing firm for the entertainment industry, and I'm conducting a survey to help determine the mid-week activities of professional adults in the Los Angeles area. Would you mind answering a few questions for me?" I had written the speech down and gone through it with just enough boredom to suggest I'd made this call at least forty times already.

"I suppose."

"Thank you, sir. I see you're an attorney in the Beverly Hills area. May I ask your income range? Between thirty to forty thousand?"

"A hundred and fifty thousand last year."

"Okay, that's box D. Are you married right now?"

"Yes."

"Is your wife employed also?"

"Self-employed."

"Did you just quote me a combined income?"

"No. She's pulling in another fifty thousand."

"Okay. Now, could you tell me what you were doing last Wednesday night, the day before yesterday?"

"I was home with my wife."

"Doing what?"

"Watching T.V."

“And what were you watching?”

“I don’t remember. Something on P.B.S.”

“How about the Wednesday before that?”

“Oh, geez. What the hell was I doing? Oh. Yeah. Same thing, only I think we rented a movie.”

“Do you remember which one?”

“Uh. No. Sorry. I probably fell asleep halfway through it, anyway.”

“Alright. Is this a usual pattern, sir?”

“Yeah. Doris and I don’t go out much during the week.”

“And that answers my next question. Thank you very much for your time, Mr. Grisom.”

I wasn’t sure if it was necessary, but I called the local Bar Association, as Mrs. Sperling had requested. The information I got was pretty interesting.

“It was years ago,” I told Mrs. Sperling as we drove to Dolores Carmine’s. “And he’s maintained an excellent record since then.”

“Embezzling, eh?”

“But they were never able to prove it. The charges were dropped before it ever went to court. The lady at the Bar Association says she remembers the incident, and she thinks it might have been professional jealousy. She says Grisom’s a terrific lawyer, and not someone you want to be facing in a divorce trial.”

“Which perhaps explains Mr. Montoinne’s caution regarding Ms. Bistler.”

“That and he’s the jealous type.”

“And Grisom’s alibi is not very easily verified,

or contested, for that matter. Relaxing at home is too common an occurrence. Sometimes a particularly strong lawyer can break the witness down, but not too often. We shouldn't count on it."

"The funny thing is, he didn't sound flustered at all, or as if he even cared whether or not I knew. If they hadn't told me about that embezzlement charge, I would have written him off, especially considering Hendricks and Bistler."

Mrs. Sperling shook her head. "Don't jump to conclusions, my dear. Something doesn't quite fit, and it could be the fact that exonerates them. One must be very sure before fixing blame."

I pulled into a parking space in front of Dolores's Gallery. We got out and went in. For once, Dolores was in the front. She waited for us with an average sized man with strong Hispanic features, and a huge bushy moustache, and long fly-away hair.

"Here he is, Delilah. He got back in town Wednesday morning," said Dolores.

Mrs. Sperling nodded. "Where have you been, Mr. Gonzagos?"

"In Mexico," he answered defensively. "I got family in Mexico City."

"Are you aware that your trip was rather poorly timed?"

"What you mean?"

"Mr. Gonzagos, the night you were last seen in Los Angeles, a man was murdered. He had been selling forgeries of prints done by the late artist, Hans Niedeman, forgeries I believe to be your work. If you arrived in back in town as Ms. Carmine here says, then you arrived just in time to be available for the murder of a second man who I believe to be the one who exchanged your prints for those of the first victim."

"I don't know nothing about no murders, lady." Gonzagos was scared. "I get mad sometimes, but I don't kill people."

"I see."

"Look, lady, you can say all you like, talk fancy and everything. But I don't kill people."

"What airlines were you on, Mr. Gonzagos?"

"Mexicana."

"Very good, then. I might also add that the second victim was severely beaten in a manner that is suggestive of your drinking habits."

Gonzagos eyes grew wide, and he darted out. I started after him, but Mrs. Sperling held me back.

"Now you done it, Delilah," growled Dolores.

"I'm afraid so. I was hoping he would make an error in judgment, but that was not the one I had in mind. Obviously, I am still capable of making mistakes. That's encouraging. Well, Dolores, thank you for getting him here."

"Delilah, maybe I shouldn't tell you this, but he says he doesn't know anything about sending a friend to me with some Niedemans to sell."

Mrs. Sperling pondered this. "Be that as it may, it still doesn't clear him, I'm afraid. Kyle Hoffman's death is too coincidental."

"Kyle Hoffman?" Dolores was shocked. "He's dead?"

"He was killed Wednesday, beaten, as I said before. You knew him?"

"Of course. He's been peddling hot art for a long time. I was beginning to think he was a fence, cause I couldn't see how he could be getting it that often for that long without getting caught."

"He may have been, but he wasn't caught due to some massive stupidity on the part of his victim."

"Must have been. Kyle's not exactly smart himself."

"Just extremely lucky. I'll be taking my leave, now, Dolores. Keep well."

"You, too, Delilah."

Mrs. Sperling was pensive as we hit the street.

"Where to now?" I asked.

"Let's check the security company, then we shall have to go home. You'll need to think up an excuse to confirm Mr. Gonzagos' flight with the airlines."

"Okey-dokey."

We got Eleanor into the car and took off. Mrs. Sperling remained distant.

"Is something wrong?" I asked.

"Yes. I just can't think what. There were two glaring mistakes in that room, two things that appeared to be as they should be but were in reality signs of an inadequate intellect. I keep running over your description of the room, and each time I come across the bird, something in my head says there's a problem with that."

"Well, you don't normally put birds next

to open windows because they get sick from draughts."

"Then we must determine why that one was there."

"Where is it now?"

"That is a good question. Remind me to ask Sergeant Michaelson when we go to the station this afternoon."

"I'll try."

At the security company, the man we wanted was in, and even better for us, working day shift at the desk. He showed us why. The cast on his leg extended to his knee.

"I was playing football with the kids over the weekend," he explained.

"That sounds quite enjoyable," replied Mrs. Sperling. "I wish I could hear more about it, but I'm afraid I don't have the time. Regarding the night, or morning, that Mr. Stein was killed..."

"Yeah, last Thursday morning."

"Did you see anything at all in the alley at any time?"

"No. I would have noted it if I had."

"I'm not talking about anything suspicious necessarily. What about things that are normally there?"

"Mr. Stein's Ferrari was there all night. And Hoffman's van, but that's always there off and on."

"What times were Mr. Hoffman's van there?"

"Just in the morning. He's there a lot in the mornings."

"Well, he was. Mr. Hoffman is no longer of this

world, I'm afraid."

"That's too bad. He wasn't a bad egg. And pretty handy, too. He fixed my air conditioner last summer. Say, you don't think he saw something, and someone bumped him off to shut him up, do you?"

"It's possible." Mrs. Sperling lapsed again. "That may be the connection." She woke up. "Thank you, sir. You've been very helpful."

"Anytime, ma'am."

Mrs. Sperling was almost prickly when we got back to the car.

"It's almost there," she grumbled. "It's within reach. I just need a little more. I'm positive the evidence is there."

"You know who the killer is?"

"I'm fairly certain I know who Hoffman's killer is, and I suspect he may be behind Stein's murder also. He's perfectly alibied for it, so he didn't actually do it. I just need a connection between him and Hoffman. It'll probably be a very loose one. He's very clever."

"He is? He must have gotten a friend to help."

Mrs. Sperling nodded.

"Are you sure the two killings are related?" I asked. "I mean the one was so perfectly staged, and the other so brutal."

"It was far more clever than that."

"It was?"

But Mrs. Sperling refused to elaborate.

At home I called a friend of mine who's a travel agent when she's not auditioning. I had to beg, plead, and practically crawl, but she relented and let me have the phone number I wanted. Mrs. Sperling listened with a great deal of amusement.

"They have a special number they use," I explained. "If I don't call that number, I'll lose a lot of credibility."

"I am aware of that. Good thinking."

I took a deep breath and misrepresented myself for the fourth time that day.

"Hello, Mexicana?" I asked. "I need a check on a passenger list, please."

"Just a minute."

Muzak floated into my ear while I waited for the right person to answer their phone.

"Yes, may I help you?" a pleasant female voice answered.

"Hi. This is Dorothy Wordsworth from William's Travel. I have a client here who claims he was billed for a round trip passage to Mexico City that he never purchased. Could you check your list and see if a Federico, or Fred Gonzagos was on a Wednesday night flight there, a week ago this Wednesday past, and returning this Wednesday morning."

"We don't have a flight leaving Los Angeles on Wednesdays."

"He said Wednesday night. Could it have been early Thursday morning?"

"Yes, it could. One moment, please. Mr. Gonzagos was on board flight 212, leaving L.A.X. at twelve-twenty A.M. He returned the following Wednesday, on flight 111, arriving L.A.X. at ten-fifteen A.M."

"Well, I guess my Mr. Gonzagos has been a victim of credit card fraud. Thank you very much." I hung up fast.

Mrs. Sperling chuckled.

"That doesn't let him off the hook," I said.

"No. But I have one more way of checking him out. Would you go find Glen for me, please?"

"Why me?" Glen asked piteously when Mrs. Sperling presented him with her plan.

"Because of those of us immediately concerned with this case, only you and Phillip DuPre have not been seen by Mr. Gonzagos. Phillip is busy and has already been in two fights. It's your turn to do some work. After all, you were the one who got me involved when you purchased that forgery." Mrs. Sperling was being unbearably reasonable.

"I'm no good at fighting," sighed Glen.

"Phil isn't either," I said.

"Here is the address." Mrs. Sperling handed him a piece of paper. "Go straight there. We'll be waiting for you at the Beverly Hills police station."

Glen left with all the enthusiasm of a former hippie signing up for selective service. I took a deep breath and looked at Mrs. Sperling.

"He's awful scared," I said. "Think he'll be able to pull it off?"

"I wouldn't have sent him if I didn't."

The phone rang and I went ahead answered it.

"Donna, just the person I want to talk to," said

Phillip's merry voice.

"Is... Um... Your video cast?"

"Yep. The producer is haggling it out with the agents. How does dinner and a movie sound tonight?"

"How does waiting around for the boss to finish her dinner sound? Mrs. Sperling is booked to go to friends. I'm driving."

"Hm. Let me think about this. Where's she dining?"

"At the Delgados, at six-thirty."

"Okay. Leave it to me. But fear not. I shan't distract you from your duties."

"You'd better not. I've got to get going. Mrs. Sperling has an appointment with Sergeant Michaelson in a little bit."

"Fine. See you tonight."

I hung up, wondering.

At the police station, I was a little surprised to see Officer Willoughby waiting with Sergeant Michaelson.

"He's here, Mrs. Sperling," said the sergeant.

"Officer Willoughby, I truly appreciate your taking your personal time to come in and talk to me."

"My pleasure, ma'am." He was lying through his teeth about that one. But then, considering what shift he worked, I couldn't really blame him.

"As I believe the sergeant told you, there were a couple points about Wednesday's incident that I believe the Hollywood police confused. Perhaps if you could tell me exactly what happened in your own words."

"Well, as I was ending my shift, Hoffman came up to me and told me he knew something about the counterfeiting that had been going on at the Stein gallery. I thought it might be important, so I agreed to go over to his house later that afternoon, after I'd gotten some sleep, and he'd gotten off work. Now here's where I goofed. I should have told Sergeant Michaelson about it, but well, I didn't 'cause I wanted to be a hero."

"That's perfectly understandable. Do go on."

"Well, I got there, and knocked on the door. That's when I saw the landlady coming from the back. Then I heard this thud, like something falling over, and a groan. So, I busted the door in. I was about to identify myself when this huge kid in a mask came at me. He had a friend a little to the back, also masked."

"How did you know your attacker was a young man when he was masked?"

Willoughby squirmed. "I-I don't know. You just do sometimes. I guess he sounded young."

"Ah. That would be it. Please, continue."

"Well, we grappled a bit. I landed a good one on his jaw, but he took it well. He came back even harder and knocked me up against the wall. That's when he and his friend ran for the back. I went after, but I didn't get there fast enough. The last I saw of them, they were going down the fire escape. I went back into the front room, and there was Kyle under the front window."

"What did you do then?"

"I checked him, and he was gone. Then I went downstairs and called Hollywood from the landlady's place. I figured I'd better not disturb anything in Kyle's place."

"How well did you know Mr. Hoffman?"

"I might have seen him around, but I never really spoke with him until that morning."

"I see. Well, thank you, Officer. You've been most kind."

"That'll be all, Willoughby," said Michaelson. He did not like the situation.

"Oh, there you are!" Glen came up, cardboard tube in hand. "I got it. It sure looks real."

He pulled a HN4, or what looked like one, out of the tube. Mrs. Sperling sniffed.

"Excellent, Glen, you've done it again," she announced.

"Huh?" Glen grimaced.

"Be seeing you folks," said Willoughby, leaving. We ignored him.

"You mean it's another fake?" groaned Glen.

"Quite so. What happened?"

"I got there, and I told him I wanted a HN4. He said he had one. He asked how I found him. I said Kyle Hoffman sent me. He said Kyle ought to know. I looked at the print and bought it."

"Thus we can eliminate Mr. Gonzagos, except as the artist behind the counterfeits." Mrs. Sperling was pleased.

"But how?" I asked.

"Our mysterious fair-haired boy had real ones to sell. Mr. Stein only had fakes. Therefore, all of

Mr. Stein's genuine serigraphs had already been exchanged, long ago, I would expect. Mr. Stein had recently obtained a new set of serigraphs, which is why Glen was able to get one. And those, too, were exchanged, with Mr. Gonzagos receiving the payment Wednesday, and deciding to go to visit his family with the cash while he had it. Then Dolores got a set of genuine Niedemans from a friend of Mr. Gonzagos, who knew nothing of him. Ergo, Mr. Gonzagos merely prints the serigraphs, for which he receives cash, and nothing else. Even if he knew Mr. Stein existed, and vice versa, which I seriously doubt, Mr. Gonzagos would have no reason to kill Mr. Stein, as he represented a form of income."

"But what about Hoffman?" asked Sergeant Michaelson.

"You know Mr. Gonzagos didn't kill Mr. Hoffman," Mrs. Sperling replied. "Besides, Mr. Gonzagos referred to Mr. Hoffman in the present. It would appear Mr. Gonzagos does not yet know Mr. Hoffman is deceased."

Michaelson shifted. "I suppose. But we still don't have the evidence, and I still don't like it."

"I don't blame you, Sergeant. It's very disheartening. However, we cannot ignore the truth because we wish it were otherwise. The evidence is coming. It's simmering on the back burner, so to speak, and the best I can do is let it find its own way out. I trust a good night's rest will do it. In the meantime, you know what to do."

"Oh, Mrs. Sperling, you wanted me to remind

you about the bird," I suddenly added.

"Oh, yes. Thank you, Donna. Sergeant, what became of the bird we found in Mr. Stein's studio? It was a parakeet, was it not?"

"Yeah, a green one. One of the lab boys took it home for his kid. As far as I know, it's alive and well."

"Good."

"Sergeant!" A young female clerk came up with a small piece of paper. "Hollywood called. They said you might want to know. Central recovered Kyle Hoffman's van this morning near Union Station."

Michaelson frowned. "I didn't know it was stolen."

"Neither did Hollywood. But Central said it had been hot-wired."

"Sergeant," interrupted Mrs. Sperling. "Would you please obtain a list of the van's contents for me? There could be something significant."

"Certainly," he said.

"Thank you, Sergeant. Glen, you'd better leave that print here as evidence. I'll see you back at the house."

"Sure." Glen dropped the tube and hurried out.

Mrs. Sperling and I followed at a more relaxed pace.

"That's enough of this for today," she sighed. "I'm going to forget about it, and rest. I've been working it too hard, that much is obvious."

"I thought you said it was critical last night."

"It is very critical, which is why I've overworked it. It happens to all of us sometimes, and the fastest way to get it done is to lay it aside for a while and forget it. The Delgados' invitation is most timely."

We went home, first, and Mrs. Sperling answered a few letters to friends while I cleaned my room. Mrs. Sperling and I didn't change for dinner. It was to be a casual affair. At six-fifteen, I brought the Lexus around.

The Delgados are usually pretty cool about letting me hang around when they are entertaining Mrs. Sperling. But Mrs. Delgado's mother had invited herself, and she isn't quite so liberal. After letting Mrs. Sperling and Eleanor off, I took the car around back and hung out in the kitchen with the cook and the butler, when he wasn't serving dinner. They were both busy and gossiping amongst themselves, which left me a little out of things. They tried to include me, but I just wasn't interested in the affair Mrs. Jones' butler was having with Mrs. Smith's gardener.

Around seven, someone knocked at the back door. Mimi, the cook, went and got it.

"Well, Mr. DuPre!" she said with pleased surprise. "What brings you back here?"

"Delilah Sperling's chauffeur," Phil answered. "We're sharing a box dinner in the car. Would you be so kind as to let us know when Mrs. Sperling wants us?"

"Sure." Mimi looked at me as if she couldn't wait to tell the butler.

"Don't worry about interrupting anything," I told her as I left. "It'll just be a friendly affair."

Phil grinned as he swept me out the rest of the way.

"You haven't eaten yet, I hope," he said.

"Mimi was going to fix me a plate after the others were settled."

"Perfect." Phil got a picnic basket and a bottle of wine from his BMW. "Why don't we dine in the Lexus? It's got more room."

"I hope Mrs. Sperling doesn't mind."

"How is she going to know?"

"She'll find a way."

"I'll take responsibility. If she doesn't accept that, then I'll have to hire you as my chauffeur."

"Hm." I unlocked the car, then opened the back door. "I must be nuts climbing into a back seat with you."

I wasn't really. Dinner came out of a basket that Phil had gotten from a restaurant. There was pate, and endive and spinach salad, then creamy vegetable soup, potatoes Lyonnaise, fresh steamed broccoli, and veal aux fines herbes provencal. He'd also picked up some vintage Chandon, brie and white chocolate chunk cookies from Trader Joe's, a local discount wine and gourmet food store. Phil has a definite cheap streak. We ate, then cleared dishes and snuggled.

One factor we didn't count on was that it had been a long week of late hours and early mornings for both of us, and that sitting in a nice warm car does induce drowsiness. I'm not sure when Phil dozed off. I know I'd been asleep for some time when Mimi came banging on the windows. Phil started and cussed. I yawned and blinked.

"She's ready," yelled Mimi.

"Who?" I grumbled. "Oh, damn!" I shook the remaining sleep from me.

Phil was already outside the car with the picnic basket. I crawled out.

"I'll see you over at Aunt Delilah's." He kissed me and was gone.

I got in the driver's seat and brought the Lexus around front. Mrs. Sperling talked with Mrs. Delgado on the drive. I got out and held open the back door. Eventually, they said goodnight, and Mrs. Sperling put Eleanor in the back seat.

"I hope your company wasn't too bad," she said as I opened the front passenger door.

"It was very pleasant." I hurried around to my side.

"It was?" Mrs. Sperling got in, shut the door, then sniffed. I shut my door and busied myself with getting my seat belt buckled and the car started. "I can imagine it was very pleasant. I was wondering why you hadn't found Mimi and Engle dreadful bores."

"He surprised me, and after he went to all that trouble..."

"I had a feeling he would. You seem to have dined well."

"I hope you don't mind. We were very careful."

"Why should I care? Eleanor has her paws all over that back seat all the time. What difference is a little food going to make? You've been doing an excellent job of keeping this car up, anyway. I'm sure I'd be the last person to notice a stain."

I giggled. "Then there's no reason to bother you about the salad oil all over the seat."

"The what?"

"Just teasing."

Mrs. Sperling laughed.

"I wouldn't try to put anything past you, anyway," I said. "There's no way I could get away with it."

"That may or may not be encouraging."

As he promised, Phil was waiting outside when I pulled into the driveway.

"Hi, Donna. Hello, Aunt Delilah." He dutifully kissed Aunt Delilah's cheek while I put the Lexus in the garage. "I just stopped by to visit with Donna after she got off duty."

"After you already spent the evening with her?" Mrs. Sperling asked, and opened the back door.

"I told you she'd find out." I walked past Phil into the house.

"It was worth a try," Phil replied.

"Then next time I would recommend cold food and something with a less distinctive smell than fines herbes." Mrs. Sperling smiled. "Is Glen home?"

"Yeah," Phil answered. "He drove in just as I did."

"Good. Donna, would you please put the burglar alarm on? I'm going to bed."

I was stopped by a series of bloodcurdling screams.

len backed up against the wall across the hallway to his room, white faced and uttering
the chilling screams. He half-pointed into his
room. I saw something dark writhing on the floor.
Without thinking, I ducked in and pulled the door
shut.

"S-s-sna... S-s-s-snakes!" Glen squeaked out.
With the immediate threat removed, his screams
reduced themselves to gasps.

"Were you bit?" Mrs. Sperling asked with calm
concern.

Glen shook his head, still gasping.

"He's as white as a ghost!" exclaimed Phil. He
slid under Glen's right arm. "We'd better get him
sat down."

I slid under Glen's other arm, and we
maneuvered him down the hall into the living
room.

"He doesn't look good, Aunt Delilah," said Phil
as we sat Glen, still gasping, on the couch. "You got
some smelling salts?"

"I think a paper bag would be more effective,"
answered Mrs. Sperling.

"I've got one in my room." I jumped up and

ran back.

As I switched on the light, I stopped. I didn't see anything, but I went in cautiously. The bag was on the escritoire. I poked at it and snapped back. Nothing. I gingerly tugged at it. It came free without anything flashing at me. I took it and hurried back to the living room.

Mrs. Sperling sat on the couch next to Glen and rubbed his back as he gasped for air. I rolled the bag back and handed it to her. She put it to his face.

"It's alright, Glen. You're safe," she whispered.

"How the hell should I know what kind?" Phil yelled into the phone. "We didn't stick around to examine them... Frankly, I don't think knocking on the door and asking is going to get much of an answer, and I'm sure as hell not opening that door... Just assume they're poisonous, will you?"

Slowly, Glen got his breathing under control. Sobs replaced the gasps, and Glen buried his head in Mrs. Sperling's shoulder.

"I'm scared to death of snakes," he sniffed.

"How many did you see?" Mrs. Sperling asked.

"There were two of them."

"What exactly happened? From the time you came home."

"I said hi to Phil and said he could wait for Donna in the house. He said he'd wait for her in the driveway. I went in and went to the bathroom, then to my room. There was one on the desk and one on the floor. The floor one came at me. I don't think he got me, though. I just got out of there fast as I could."

"Snakes usually hibernate this time of year. He was probably slow and sleepy." Mrs. Sperling's hands examined Glen's shoe. "There are two puncture holes here on the toe."

I had the loafer and sock off in less than a second.

"His foot's fine," I sighed with relief.

"You're very lucky," said Mrs. Sperling.

"I don't want to think about it," Glen wailed. He swore. "I must look like an ass, crying like a baby."

"Not at all, dear." Mrs. Sperling rocked him. "It's an understandable phobia, and with the shock and the narrow escape, tears are more than justified. Better to get it out than more firmly entrench the fear by holding your emotions in."

"It takes a lot more guts to express it," added Phil, who had just hung up. "The police will be here in a minute, with a poisonous snake crew as soon as they can find one. The jackasses. They wanted me to be sure the snakes were poisonous first."

"Given the rarity of the specialty needed, I suppose it's not entirely unwarranted," sighed Mrs. Sperling. "It is rather incredible that poisonous snakes should be found loose in a house located in a crowded neighborhood. Glen, do you think any of your friends would go to such an extreme to play a joke on you?"

"No."

"I don't think so, either. This could be

considered a warning."

"But why Glen?" I asked.

"His is the only open window in the house."

"Aunt Delilah, maybe you guys oughta go to a hotel tonight," suggested Phil.

"We'll see what happens when the police arrive. If this was a warning, then I expect the miscreant will give us some time not to act upon it. Furthermore, he'll need time to develop a plan."

The doorbell rang. I got up to get it, but Mrs. Sperling held me back and sent Phil instead.

It was the police, two uniformed officers and a detective who knew Mrs. Sperling. They took our statements and looked at the closed door to Glen's room. Mrs. Sperling sent Phil and me into the kitchen to make herb tea for everyone to drink while we waited for the snake crew to arrive.

"Are you okay?" Phil asked as I filled a kettle with water.

"I suppose," I sighed. "I am feeling a little creepy crawly, but I agree with Mrs. Sperling that running is pointless. I think it's better to take a stand and show we won't be cowed."

"Not if it gets you killed. I think I'm going to spend the night. Someone ought to stand guard."

"You're crazy, Phil. Is there a teapot around here? I thought I saw a nice ceramic one... Oh, here it is. If you're going to spend the night, you'd better ask Mrs. Sperling. It's her house."

"I will," Phil replied belligerently.

"Fine. Will you help me get some cups out and on this tray. Oh, and let's put these cookies out.

Mrs. Sperling likes the arrowroot biscuits."

It was another ten minutes before the water boiled. Phil and I brought two trays and the teapot into the living room just as the snake crew arrived. They were actually an animal control team, one of whose members specialized in handling snakes. He was dressed in heavy boots, gloves and a loose canvas jumpsuit, and carried a forked stick with a loop of rope hanging off the end. His partner handed him a burlap bag, and the two went back to Glen's room. They came out a few minutes later with a squirming sack and few nice words.

"Diamondbacks," said the snake handler.

"Those are rattlesnakes." Mrs. Sperling looked surprised. "We didn't hear anything."

"They've had their rattles cut off."

"Ah. The Synanon affair. That was some time ago. Our miscreant has some memory."

"That's not very encouraging," I grumbled.

The snake handler gave his sack to his partner, then beckoned the two uniformed officers.

"We'd better search the house. One or two could have escaped the room."

Glen let out a strangled little moan. I grabbed the paper bag lest he start hyperventilating again. He calmed himself and I relaxed. It was another hour before the search was over. It had been very thorough, and nothing was found. Even Glen was reassured. By the time everyone had left, he was walking around, and his color had returned.

"I say it's high time we were in bed," said Mrs. Sperling. "Glen, why don't you sleep upstairs in the guest room tonight?"

"I'd totally like that," he sighed in relief.

"Fine. Donna, would you please fetch his nightclothes and anything else he might need?"

"Sure. Glen?"

"Just my pajamas. They're under my pillow."

"Aunt Delilah, I think I'd better stick around," said Phil. "I don't have anything to do but sleep tomorrow, and I can keep an eye on things just in case."

"It really isn't necessary, Phillip. But if it will make you feel better, you may."

I left to get Glen's pajamas and was back in an instant. Shortly after, I was in my sleep t-shirt, heading for bed. I don't like admitting it, but I was scared. I knew the animal control people had searched every nook and cranny. They'd even gone through my bed linens. But something in the back of my mind kept whispering "What if...?"

I heard Phil pacing in the living room. I shut my door and went to bed. Alright. I did leave my light on, and I did poke through the bed linens, and I searched under the bed, and I went through my closet. But I was scared.

I awoke around eight thirty the next morning. Silence reigned. It was eerie, given the night before. I couldn't go back to sleep. I got up and took a shower and got dressed. I went past the living room to get to the kitchen. Phil's black hit-tops sat next to the couch. A loud rumbling growl broke the calm of the morning.

I looked closer and saw Phil sprawled on his

back along the length of the couch with his lower legs falling off the end. His mouth opened and another monstrous snore escaped. I giggled.

I went on to the kitchen. The rumble came again, softer but still distinct enough to be remarked upon, even in the kitchen.

Mrs. Osgood bustled in.

"Something is funny?" she asked. Phil rumbled again. "What in Heaven's name is that? The pipes are bad again?"

I laughed. "It's Phil DuPre. He's asleep on the couch. We had quite a time here last night."

Mrs. Osgood's eyes twinkled. "So that is why you are smiling."

"No!" I blushed, then told her about the snakes.

"In Jamaica, we say that is bad magic. But Mrs. Sperling, she is a good woman. No evil can harm us in her house." She took off her coat and hung it in the broom closet as was her custom. Mrs. Sperling has suggested she use the hall closet, but Mrs. Osgood prefers the broom closet for reasons known only to her. Though usually merry and good-tempered, Mrs. Osgood has her temperamental side, and all of us in Mrs. Sperling's house would fain cross her.

Glen appeared next, in good spirits despite the previous night's trauma.

"How long before brunch, Mrs. Osgood?" he asked.

"Eleven, as usual."

"That's an hour from now." Glen looked at me. I was at the table drinking orange juice and looking at Facebook on my phone. "Is it okay if I make some toast?"

"Certainly." Mrs. Osgood made carrot bits faster than a Cuisinart.

Glen dodged her gracefully, fetching bread, butter, and homemade jam from the refrigerator. A muffled obscenity emerged from the living room. A minute later, Phil wandered in, his hair tousled, his chin bristly, and eyes blinking.

"I fell asleep," he grumbled.

"No kidding," I replied. "They probably heard you snoring down at the Beverly Hills police station."

Phil yawned. "I must have been beat. I don't normally do that unless I'm really tired."

"How would you know? You live alone."

"I haven't always. Splice-Man has some tales that could stand your hair on end. At least he claims that's what I did to him a couple times. Is Aunt Delilah up yet?"

"I don't know," said Glen. "I didn't hear anything when I got up, and I showered down here. And, Donna, could you please quit throwing your shavers into the sink when you're done with them? You totally missed again, and I almost sliced my foot up."

"I don't want to slice myself up in the shower. I'll try and be more careful."

"Maybe we'd better check on her," said Phil.

Glen looked up at the ceiling. "There goes the shower now. She must be okay."

"Must be," sighed Phil.

"Would you like some orange juice and toast?" I asked. "It'll be a while before the rest of it's ready."

"No thanks." Phil stretched and got out his keys. "I want to get showered and changed myself. I'll be back in a jiffy. Where are my shoes? Oh."

He left for the living room and came back shod a minute later. He kissed me goodbye and took off.

Carrot bran muffins, salmon souffle, steamed zucchini, and buttered new potatoes steamed on the table when Phil got back.

"You look a lot better," I said as he walked in.

"I probably smell a lot better, too." He sat down. "It looks terrific, Mrs. Osgood."

"Thank you."

"Where's Aunt Delilah?"

"Right here." Mrs. Sperling walked in wearing a dark brown shaggy sweater and black slacks.

"Oh no," sighed Glen. "Did those policemen mess up your closet, Mrs. Sperling?"

"I don't believe so. These are my black pants, aren't they?" Her fingers slid around to her back, lifting up the sweater and feeling under the waistband.

"Yes. But you're wearing your brown sweater. Black and brown don't go together."

Mrs. Sperling froze. "That's right. They don't. Glen, what color socks would you wear with brown pants?"

"Brown."

"Not black?"

Glen made a disgusted face. "Yuck."

"And what would you say about someone who wore black socks with brown pants?"

"I'd say he totally had no taste."

"Phillip, would you say the same?"

"Perhaps not in those words, but yeah."

"And yet we know that Mr. Stein was particular about his appearance and a stylish dresser. But Mr. Hoffman wasn't. In fact, he wore white socks with a suit to Mr. Stein's funeral."

"I don't get it," I said.

"Well, I do, at long last." Mrs. Sperling chuckled. "My subconscious was certainly at work when I got dressed this morning. That was the other glaringly stupid mistake that I was wondering about. Now the bird fits in perfectly, and my goodness, the pajamas, too!"

Glen gave up at that point, rolling his eyes heavenward.

"Donna, we'll need to call that gentleman in that lone occupied office in the building that Mr. Stein's gallery was in," Mrs. Sperling said as she picked up the phone and started dialing. "Good morning, Sergeant, I've got it... Yes, definitely... I think two would be good. I've got to double check some of the records... You did? Excellent... Please... The box... A receipt with date and time? How utterly perfect... The dead bird, too. Good. You may want it autopsied. It's pretty conclusive as it is, but it could cinch things in court... I'll be having something double checked in a minute, but it's far simpler than we originally thought, and yet more complicated... The case against him is still a little circumstantial, but it's the best I can do. At the very least, we have enough to hold him then get a search warrant... Very good, then. We'll see you at two." She hung up with a very pleased look on her face.

I read her the number for the office she wanted. The call was relatively short, with most of the discussion taking place on the other end. Mrs. Sperling I see'd a lot, then hung up looking pretty well satisfied with herself.

She instructed me to pull the Bug convertible around, with the top down.

"It's pretty cloudy out there," I warned.

"We'll risk it," she said, smiling.

She hurried off to get Eleanor's harness.

Glen and Phil came along for the ride. Phil rode up front with me, while Glen squeezed in back with Mrs. Sperling and Eleanor. From Mrs. Sperling's gay mood, you would have thought we were off to a party.

Sergeant Michaelson was yet again waiting for us.

"I thought I'd save you the trouble," he told Mrs. Sperling. "I checked those reports, and you were right. He made a stop on July seventh."

"Which corresponds exactly with the date Hoffman left the Hendricks building. Perfect."

"He also stopped on the day of the murder. I got that management company to send me a copy of Hoffman's application. Guess who Hoffman named as a reference?"

"Even better. The District Attorney should be

pleased."

"Hi, Sergeant." Willoughby came up, in civvies and looking rested.

"I'm glad you're here, Officer Willoughby," said Mrs. Sperling pleasantly. "I wanted to double check your story."

"I thought you did." Willoughby frowned.

"Not the Hoffman story. The one you wrote in your report on July seventh of this year. You stopped and left your car to investigate something suspicious in the alley behind the art gallery owned by Mr. Edgar Hendricks. You reported back ten minutes later, saying you hadn't found anything except a nesting cat."

"Yeah. I think I remember that. So?"

"I believe that nesting cat you saw was Mr. Kyle Hoffman removing art works from Mr. Hendricks gallery. It's strange how Mr. Hendricks' overload of back orders ceased to increase after that date, and even stranger how Mr. Hoffman suddenly quit and went to work for the company that manages Mr. Stein's building. Would you care to elaborate?"

Willoughby remained cool, but I could see he was scared.

"No, I wouldn't," he replied, folding his arms in front of him.

"I didn't think you would, so I will." Mrs. Sperling's smile was a little grim. "Mr. Hendricks began getting full orders of prints. Mr. Stein also received full orders, but several of the prints he sold turned out to be counterfeit. They were mostly inexpensive serigraphs and lithos. That's why they went unnoticed until my houseboy, Glen, here, purchased an HN4 by Hans Niedeman, and I discovered it was a fake. Phillip told me that Mr. Stein knew about the counterfeits. You had already engineered the counterfeiting scheme, being careful to make sure it was Kyle Hoffman who contacted Mr. Fred Gonzagos and purchased his work, and Mr. Hoffman who switched the serigraphs. It was quite simple to remain the brains behind the operation. Until Mr. Hoffman discovered Mr. Stein's body in his studio. You see, there was a carbon monoxide leak in the forced air system late the day before that forced Mr. Hoffman to shut the building down while he tried to fix the problem. The owner of Best Rentals left promptly. We must assume that Mr. Stein was not in his gallery when Mr. Hoffman shut the building down. And we must assume that Mr. Hoffman was not aware that Mr. Stein was sleeping in the back room of the gallery, thanks to having left his wife but a few days before. Mr. Stein had apparently returned to his gallery with his evening's dinner and finished most of it. He was probably beginning to feel woozy and sleepy. Carbon monoxide generally acts fast. He changed into his pajamas and fell, striking the back of his head. Early the next morning, Hoffman flagged you down, Officer Willoughby. He was panicking. Stein was dead, and Mr. Hoffman would lose his job, putting both himself and your schemes in peril. You decided to make it appear as though Mr. Stein been dumped there after having been killed in a car in someone's garage, which is what we indeed thought. You had Mr. Hoffman air out the studio and set up the counterfeiting scene. Mr. Hoffman failed miserably there, setting up insufficient equipment and a genuine serigraph. That really didn't matter in the long run. However, there were two problems. Either you or Mr. Hoffman apparently noticed that Mr. Stein's parakeet had died, as it would be expected to do quite quickly when the carbon monoxide laden exhaust came into the room. I'm not sure when one of you retrieved the dead bird, but Mr. Hoffman did purchase another, unfortunately leaving the receipt, with date and time stamped on it, and the carry home box in his van for us to find later. There was also the pajama situation. You told Hoffman to change Mr. Stein into regular clothes. Hoffman, taking no chances took the pajamas and all of Mr. Stein's other nightclothes, and disposed of them, assuming we'd notice that the one set of pajamas were missing, and thus discover what had really happened. Mr. Hoffman made one mistake, though. He knew that a stylish man like Mr. Stein would wear dark socks with dark pants, but he put black socks on with brown pants, something we know Mr. Stein would never have done." She looked at Sergeant Michaelson. "That's what took so long to come out for me. I had forgotten that black and brown are not generally compatible colors."

"Something I believe we can't fault you for," Sergeant Michaelson replied with a grim smile.

"In any case, Mr. Hoffman also put the purchased bird into the birdcage, and not willing to make the same mistake again, put the cage next to the window, so as not to poison the new bird. All was ready in the studio, and Mr. Hoffman went up to the roof to finish the repairs to the vent system."

"Okay," said Willoughby. "I can see Hoffman doing that. But I don't see where you come off saying I put him up to it."

"Somebody had to be doing Hoffman's thinking for him. The plan was too subtle, too refined, and it was generally acknowledged that Mr. Hoffman was not terribly bright, although handy with environmental systems. In addition, a young man sold an art dealer in Hollywood five genuine Niedeman serigraphs invoking Fred Gonzagos' name, even though he was in Mexico at the time. The man was described as tall and light-haired, which you cannot deny you are."

"No, but look at your houseboy, and Mr. Director there."

"True, it's a common description, but it does not fit any friends of Mr. Gonzagos, at least none that he's recommended to Dolores Carmine. You obviously knew about Mr. Gonzagos, even if he did not know about you. You probably found his record and recommended that Mr. Hoffman seek him out. Then you sold the serigraphs when you decided that they might be damaging to you. It's an interesting coincidence, too, that Mr. Stein's locker at his health club was cleared out by a tall light-haired young man the day I handed in a report to Sergeant Michaelson, which you saw, and in which I mentioned a curiosity about Mr. Stein's toiletries at the afore mentioned club. Then there was Hoffman's death, which also occurred the same day. Your story of the punks in the apartment fit the evidence perfectly. Too perfectly. Everything was exactly as the police could expect to find it, as you've undoubtedly found it many times. But there were no physical traces left behind, such as a smudged print, or a torn button. The only people who leave the scene of the crime that clean are professional burglars, and they wouldn't bother with a place like Hoffman's. But what really tipped me off was Mrs. Parrish's story. She said when she saw you, you just went in. Later she assumed you had broken the door in because it was broken, but not at first. Her eyes hadn't fooled her the first time. Hoffman had admitted you. So, I knew you had lied. I caught you again when you said the punks went down the fire escape. Perhaps Mr. Hoffman mentioned leaving it open. But you made the same mistake my chauffeur did. You assumed the fire escape was a balcony affair when it was actually a window that opened wide enough to facilitate escape. You also referred to the corpse, saying 'there was Kyle.' indicating you knew him much better than you claimed."

Willoughby swallowed. "It's circumstantial. It'll never hold water in court."

"I'm sorry, Willoughby," said Sergeant Michaelson. "We've got enough evidence to swear out a search warrant for your apartment."

"You can't!" Willoughby's face went white.

"Where he will find all the other stolen artworks from various galleries and homes in the area that you have managed to acquire through all your various schemes," finished Mrs. Sperling.

Sergeant Michaelson sighed as he read. "Willoughby, you have the right to remain silent…"

Did that one ever make the headlines. The search warrant turned up over five million dollars' worth of stolen property in Willoughby's apartment. According to the D.A.'s office, at least five different fraud and theft scams were accounted for by the loot, including one where the victim didn't even know his stuff had been taken.

Mrs. Sperling managed to stay out of the newspapers, as usual. But my family figured out who the "private citizen" was and insisted on details when Phil and I went over there for dinner that Sunday. We diplomatically omitted the snake incident.

As for that, Willoughby just happened to be off duty that night and unable to prove his whereabouts all evening. They also dug up an old record that showed Willoughby had been in on the arrest of some guys who had stolen the snakes from a trainer. The trainer had never gotten them back, and it was assumed the snakes had been lost, until, of course, they showed in Glen's bedroom. All I have to do is whisper snake, and Glen still turns pale.

Stein's will got through probate without a

hitch, fortunately or unfortunately, depending on how you feel about Ramona Bistler. She didn't really give a damn about Willoughby getting caught, but Edgar Hendricks was very relieved to know he was off the hook. It turned out that the night of the murder they were together in Ventura, which accounted for Bistler's empty gas tank. They were trying to keep it a secret because of the money. They moved in together right away in spite of Montoinne's objections. I understand Mrs. Sperling had a little chat with Ms. Bistler the day Willoughby was arrested.

The building that Stein's gallery had been in was eventually sold. I heard later that the owner of Best Rentals had decided to work out of his house.

We never did find out what Devon and Stein had been arguing about. Devon was delighted that he didn't have to pay for the broken pottery after all. He hadn't even been aware that he'd been suspected. As for seeing him those two nights, well, he really is everywhere. Gillian quit and moved to New York. Devon tried to offer me the job, but I preferred the one I had.

Tina, Mickey, and I all got cast in the video. We had a blast shooting it. Phil and Mickey are getting to be pretty good friends, too. Mickey's stint at the Laugh Factory was a smash. He got held over and signed again for another stint later the next year. Tina keeps teasing Phil and asking when he's shooting his next video. Phil's casting one right now, but he doesn't need any dancers. I told Tina I wasn't even getting cast, and she said that didn't matter.

I've been working. I did a guest star spot, and I've got a second lead in a film that starts shooting this spring in the Bahamas. Mrs. Sperling "just happened" to decide to visit her parents in Japan the five weeks I needed to do it.

I never did get another car. Phil kept joking around about buying me a new one, until my mother threatened to crown him. Other than that, my parents love Phil, even though they know he's in showbiz. Dad heard about Phil's real estate investments and was thrilled.

Glen got his HN4 eventually. Mrs. Sperling broke down and bought it for him for his birthday, which was right after Thanksgiving.

"Are you sure it's real?" he asked her.

"Of course," she replied. "The nose knows, doesn't it?"

Coming Soon

The next Mrs. Sperling mystery isn't written yet. So, I have a sneak peek at the sequel to the popular Death of the Zanjero, set in Old Los Angeles, 1870, and featuring Maddie Wilcox. Death of the City Marshal is based on a real historical event. Enjoy.

Death of the City Marshal

When the shooting stopped and the smoke cleared, there were five people bearing wounds from the bullets that had flown so fast and furiously. I had made a point of diving for cover the moment I'd seen City Marshal William Warren pull his derringer from behind his back. Most of the other women in front of the Clocktower Courthouse that fateful afternoon of October 31, the Year of Our Lord 1870, had quickly left the street for some safe indoor place the moment they'd heard Deputy Joe Dye screaming at Marshal Warren. The men and I stayed to see the show.

My father often said that I didn't have the sense that God gave a goose. However, in my defense, I must point out that the closest indoor cover was a saloon, from which those of my fair sex were barred, and that any effort to seek cover across the street in the market on the first floor of the courthouse would have been impeded by the crowd that was gathering. I was looking for some other safe haven when I saw the marshal's derringer and decided that down on the board walkway was safer than anywhere I could reach.

As I rose, I was not surprised to see the marshal and a Chinaman on the ground and bleeding. What did surprise me was that Mr. Dye was bleeding from his forehead and his leg, but so enraged was he that he had pounced upon Marshal Warren and was biting his ear. Two men, I did not see who, grabbed Mr. Dye by the throat, and pulled him off the Marshal. Deputy Jose Redona was easing onto the ground, a bullet hole in his upper right arm. Deputy Constable Robert Hester was bent over his bleeding right hand. The young Chinawoman Marshal Warren and Mr. Dye had been fighting over sat huddled near Mr. Hester, too frightened to move.

I went first to the Chinaman and saw that the bullet had struck his jaw. I grabbed some bandages from the huge bag I always wore and began to gently bind his head, but another Chinaman eased me away and took over. So I went over to Marshal Warren.

"I'm killed," he groaned.

"Not if I have anything to say about it," I told him.

I began to bandage the nether region above his limbs in spite of his embarrassment. I did not like doing so in public, but he was bleeding and the bandage was necessary.

Perhaps I should explain. My name is

Madeline Franklin Wilcox, called Maddie by my intimate friends, and I am a trained medical doctor. Nowadays, sadly, a woman medical doctor is almost unheard of, but when I finished my training in 1859, it was not all that unusual, though still fairly rare. My father had been so ashamed of me he forced me to marry Albert Wilcox, who promptly dragged me here to Los Angeles, then still a tiny pueblo of five thousand people. Mr. Wilcox bought a vineyard and promptly died, leaving me to make my way as a winemaker who happened to have a talent for the healing arts. I'd been forced to finally reveal myself as a doctor the previous spring. Not everyone, including Marshal Warren, was entirely comfortable with my true vocation.

Marshal Warren was an average-sized man with dark hair and eyes and an overgrown and unruly mustache and beard of the sort that was favored by men of that time. We'd never gotten on well. However, we had developed a grudging respect for each other, and if he did not appear happy that it was me that had come to his aid, at least he wasn't fighting me.

Four men took the marshal on ahead to his house. I told them that I would be there as soon as I checked on Mr. Redona and Mr. Hester. Mr. Hester's wound was superficial and barely needed bandaging. Doc MacKenzie was tending to Mr. Redona. Mr. Redona called out to me. He, apparently, had as little confidence in Doc MacKenzie as I did.

It wasn't entirely fair. Doc MacKenzie had many years of experience, even if he had no formal training. And he would give me the benefit of the doubt, which was more than the other doctors in town would. Fortunately, that day, we were both in agreement that the bullet had passed through Mr. Redona's arm without harming the bone and little more needed to be done beyond stitching the holes shut. I told Mr. Redona to keep the wound clean (which also served to remind Doc MacKenzie that sanitation was of the utmost importance). Then I hurried off to the marshal's house to tend to him.

Mrs. Warren was waiting for me as I ran up. Doctor Skillen came running up and glared at me. He generally approved of me when I tended to the women and children in town. However, he firmly believed that I had no business treating men. But Mrs. Warren told him in no uncertain terms that she wanted me tending to her husband and sent him off.

"How is he?" I asked Mrs. Warren as she led me upstairs.

"Complaining like a little girl," she said, then frowned. "That's good, isn't it?"

"Usually, yes," I said, not wanting to say more.

The case could go either way, based on what I'd seen on the street. He'd been hit in the pelvis. Had the bullet pierced his belly, we would have been facing a long night that would end in a slow, painful death for the marshal.

As it was, I was able to dose him with some

morphine and ether, then opened up the wound. The bullet had landed next to his bladder. I got it out, then stitched the wound up, then cleaned and stitched his ear. You'll note, I did not sterilize anything. We didn't yet know. Mr. Lister's and Mr. Pasteur's work had yet to reach our benighted little corner of the world. All I knew was that keeping things clean made it less likely that wounds would fester. I was considered somewhat radical because I used ether and morphine to dull the pain of surgery.

It was a good two hours before I was done. My work apron was a mess, but it couldn't be helped. Fortunately, Juanita, my maid and confidant, worked miracles with blood stains. I was equally happy that I had on my third best riding habit that day, a somewhat faded cotton and wool suit festooned with ruffles around the skirt. I finished washing my hands to find that Mrs. Warren had brought a guest into the room.

He was a tall man, his dark hair neatly combed as it curled slightly around his ears. His eyes were bright blue and rather striking, actually. He wore the usual dark suit which looked fairly new, although there was some dust from the street on it.

"Reverend Jeptha Bennett, Ma'am," he said, nodding at me. His voice was deep and he had a Yankee accent even thicker than my own. "I helped carry the marshal home and have stayed to help bear up Mrs. Warren and the marshal in prayer and spiritual comfort."

"That's kind of you, Reverend," I said, glancing at Mrs. Warren.

She was small and dainty, with a narrow face that often reminded me of a cat. Her hair was coal black, as were her eyes. She was a Mexican, and as such, a Catholic. I'd heard the marshal was, too. Which meant that the Reverend's offer was more kindly meant than practical.

I'd been hearing about Reverend Bennett through the previous months, although I hadn't yet met him. He supposedly espoused the fire and brimstone kind of religion that I do not hold with at all. A traveling preacher, he'd arrived in the pueblo in the middle of the summer and his revival meetings had become so popular, he'd decided to stay indefinitely.

"Father Jimenez is on his way," Mrs. Warren told me, eyeing the reverend with mild annoyance.

"It's a pleasure to finally meet you, Reverend Bennett," I said, returning to cleaning my surgical tools for a couple minutes and hoping he'd recognize this as the dismissal it was. He did not, so I turned to him. "Reverend, I would like to speak to Mrs. Warren privately, if I may?"

"Of course." The reverend bowed his head slightly and left the room.

"How bad is it?" Mrs. Warren asked the second he was gone.

"The good news is that the surgery went well," I said. "We'll have to see if he takes sick from it. We should know in a few hours. I'll wait here with you."

"Thank you, Mrs. Wilcox," she said, going over and stroking her husband's face. "Oh, Mr. Ortiz came by. He thought you might be here and said to tell you that he will tell Mrs. Ortiz not to expect you for dinner."

I couldn't help smiling. I didn't know whether Mr. Ortiz meant Sebastiano or Enrique. They were the brothers who helped me manage my property, with Sebastiano overseeing the winery and Enrique the vineyards. They had started as my workers, but we had become fast friends and I'd recently made them my partners. Their wives managed my household, with Enrique's wife Magdalena as the housekeeper and Sebastiano's wife Olivia as the cook. It didn't matter which of the two brothers had delivered the message to Mrs. Warren, it was clear they knew me well.

"That was a kindness," I said and went back to cleaning tools. "Are your daughters at home?"

Mrs. Warren's three girls were still fairly young.

"Their grandmother is here but can take them to her house at any time."

I glanced over at the marshal, who stirred. "I'm hopeful, but best keep them close."

Mrs. Warren nodded, her eyes filling with tears. She knew as well as I did what peril the marshal was in, and that it would be best for the girls to be able to say goodbye to their father if need be. Still, he was breathing evenly and his color was good for his condition.

I grew more hopeful as the afternoon wore

on. Father Jimenez arrived and sat next to the window, muttering over his beads. Marshal Warren mostly slept. He awoke once just before sunset, chided me briefly, then went back to sleep again. Outside the house, several of the marshal's friends ambled back and forth, waiting.

Mr. Leander Wills, a notary of the local court, came by after dusk to get the marshal's testimony for the court's examination of Deputy Dye, which would be the next day. Mr. Wills was so insistent, I could hear him all the way upstairs. I told Mrs. Warren to wait with her husband and went to the front door.

Mr. Wills was a small man with a rounded belly and pince-nez glasses. He was meticulously clean-shaven and his suits were hand-tailored of the best wool, and his vests usually a shade of blue or yellow. He was wearing one the color of marigolds that evening.

"I am here as an officer of the court," he announced. "I must get the marshal's testimony."

"I'm afraid you're not going to get it," I told him. "The marshal is asleep and neither I nor anyone else, is going to wake him."

Mr. Wills' eyes narrowed. Standing behind him was Mr. King, one of the two men who ran The Daily News. Mr. King did most of the reporting for the newspaper. Mr. Wills harrumphed a couple times. I continued to glare at him. Mr. Wills harrumphed one more time then turned away from the door. As I shut it, I saw him shrug at the reporter.

Half an hour later, Constable Hester came by to visit and was able to speak briefly with the marshal, as did Deputy Redona.

"You should be in bed," I told the deputy. "You could still take sick from that hole in your arm."

Deputy Redona laughed loudly and the smell of whiskey washed over me. It was patently obvious how Doc MacKenzie had chosen to dull Mr. Redona's pain.

"It'll take more than this little hole to knock me down," Deputy Redona said, his body listing slightly to the right.

Deputy Redona did leave shortly after, promising to return, and left Constable Hester in the front parlor to watch. Reverend Bennett stayed with them. Father Jimenez had stayed until dinner time. In fairness, it didn't look like the marshal was going to need last rites. When the family's eight-day clock struck ten that night, I checked the marshal for fever, found he didn't have one, then motioned Mrs. Warren outside the room.

"I can't say for sure that he's out of danger," I told her. "You know as well as I do, wounds can look perfectly all right, then all of a sudden start festering. But I do think it's unlikely at this point. If you want me to stay, I'll be happy to. However, I see little point in it."

"I don't either," she said, looking through the door at her husband. "He just needs rest."

"As do I," I said. "If anything changes, don't wait to send for me. But I'll be back by dawn.

Would it be all right if I didn't knock? I don't want to wake anyone unnecessarily."

"Oh, please, just come straight in."

I returned to the room to gather my bag and other things. I almost always carried a large leather bag, not unlike a saddle bag, with me wherever I went. The long strap crossed over my chest and wore my dresses terribly. However, I had my surgical tools and my most useful drugs with me at all times. The gunplay that we'd seen earlier that day was all too common, along with knife fights and other forms of violence. Even if it weren't, malaria, assorted poxes, and scarlet fever lurked everywhere, not to mention typhoid and cholera. Then there were the accidents from runaway horses or cattle or in the mills or on the farms and vineyards surrounding our tiny pueblo. I never knew when I'd be called to the side of an ailing ranch hand or child or young mother struggling to give birth. It was best to keep my most-used remedies and tools with me.

I had folded the work apron into the bag and looked, at least, mostly presentable as I left the Warren house. The crowd outside had lessened to around five or six men. Armando Ortiz, Enrique's eldest son and a strapping youth who had just turned sixteen, was lounging on the porch. He bounced to his feet the second he saw me.

"Tío had me bring the buggy for you," he said softly in Spanish.

"That's a mercy," I replied in the same language. I had already seen the conveyance, hitched to my roan mare, Daisy, and tied up outside the house.

"Tía Olivia says that she will have soup ready for you when we get home." Armando helped me onto the trap's seat, then pulled himself up and took the reins.

Daisy ambled her way along the street toward my vineyard, winery and home, Rancho de las Flores. The wheel on the buggy squeaked exceptionally loudly and I made a mental note to ask Enrique about it when I saw him.

"I hope she will not be too put out if I'm not hungry," I said. "Señora Lopez made sure that there was plenty of food and insisted that I have some."

Señora Lopez was Mrs. Warren's mother. The Lopez family was one of our more distinguished. They had vast holdings in the area and raised cattle for beef, tallow, and hides. I can't remember if Mrs. Warren was from the third or fourth generation since the family had settled here, but they'd been here almost from the founding of the pueblo in 1781.

Armando shrugged. We both knew that Olivia considered my care and feeding her personal domain and it was equally likely that she would resent the interference from someone else as it was that she'd be grateful that someone had actually taken care of it. Heaven knows, she did not trust me to see to feeding myself, alas, with some justice on her part.

Olivia was waiting on the outside porch of the adobe as Armando and I drove in through the gate of the ranch. The adobe where I and the Ortiz families lived was not far from the gate and across the yard was the huge barn which was our winery. There was a livestock barn just beyond that, which housed Daisy, a pair of mules, a family of goats, and the three ranch dogs. The chickens had a good-sized coop closer to the barracks house, where most of our ranch hands and their families lived.

Armando helped me down off the trap's seat, then went to lock the ranch gate. I tried to read Olivia's mood. It was not an easy task. However sweet and even merry her heart was, Olivia's face was permanently set in a scowl. Her black hair was sprinkled with gray and her dark eyes were the one clue to whether there would be a tongue lashing in store for me or not.

That night, the soup she had prepared had actually been made in advance of the morning's breakfast, as the weather was turning cold and we'd even had some solid rain the week before.

"I knew Señora Lopez would feed you," Olivia said as she ushered me inside the adobe. "She's a good woman."

Olivia sniffed as if to add that however good a woman Señora Lopez was, her food couldn't possibly match Olivia's.

"It wasn't as good as I'd have gotten here," I said, dutifully.

Sebastiano, who ran our winery, was waiting for me in the front parlor, which opened directly onto the yard. He was about average size, with broad shoulders and a drooping black mustache. I can't remember if it had started to go gray by that time or if that happened later. His dark eyes usually flashed with good humor, but that night, he was not happy.

"We found two more barrels," he told me.

I bit back the foul words that sprang to my mind. "Two? How many more could there be?"

Sebastiano shrugged. Just over a week before, yet another group of young men had broken into the winery and tainted several barrels of the brandy we'd distilled the year before to make our angelica. It was the local sherry that was made all over the area, although ours was considered among the best. With the harvest done and that year's grapes mostly done fermenting, we needed the brandy to add to the new wine to fortify it so that it kept better.

We were, sadly, quite frequently the target of such vandalism. Sometimes it was from competitors. But mostly it came from men who believed a woman had no place owning a business, never mind that I had no other means of support. Even though I was getting some money for my doctoring services by then, it was hardly enough to keep me in bandages, let alone support my sizable household.

"We have enough good barrels for this year's wine," Sebastiano said. "But just enough."

"I'm assuming you made sure that they are soundly locked up?"

"Naturamente."

I thought for a moment. "Are the chickens locked in their coop?"

"Sí. You want to let the dogs loose in the yard?"

"It can't hurt."

Sebastian smiled. "I was about to suggest it."

"I'm afraid I've got to get to bed," I said, trying to stifle a yawn. "I told Mrs. Warren I'd get back to the marshal by first light."

"So he's likely to live a while longer?" Sebastiano said, his face rather neutral. He did not like the marshal, with good reason, alas, but he was too kind a man to wish anyone ill.

"It looks that way but we both know how fast that could turn."

I went on to bed. As I had planned, I was up well before the sun. Sebastiano had risen, also, and gotten my roan mare, Daisy, saddled for me. I thanked him and trotted off. The first rays were lightening the sky as I approached the door. The household was still asleep. Deputy Redona snored softly from the sofa in the front parlor. I slid upstairs quietly. Mrs. Warren was asleep in her daughters' room. Senora Lopez had, apparently, gone home.

I knew the second I entered the marshal's bedroom that something was amiss. The covers around him were completely rumpled as if he'd been struggling. A pillow lay at his feet. The marshal's eyes were wide open and he was dead.

Connect with
Anne Louise Bannon

Thank you for sticking it out this long! Please join my newsletter. It's the best way to stay up-to-date on my upcoming projects, blog posts and even games and giveaways.

Sign up here: http://eepurl.com/zH0Ab

Or connect with me on your favorite social media platforms:

Visit my website: http://annelouisebannon.com
Friend me on Facebook: http://facebook.com/RobinGoodfellowEnt
Follow me on Twitter: http://twitter.com/ALBannon
Favorite my Smashwords author page: https://www.smashwords.com/profile/view/MsBriscow
Connect on LinkedIn: http://www.linkedin.com/in/annelouisebannon
Follow me on Pinterest: http://pinterest.com/msbriscow

Other books by Anne Louise Bannon

I'm so glad you liked this book! Check out my other novels, available in print or ebook at your favorite retailer:

Freddie and Kathy Series:
Fascinating Rhythm
Bring Into Bondage
The Last Witnesses
Blood Red

Operation Quickline Series
That Old Cloak and Dagger Routine
Stopleak
Deceptive Appearances
Fugue in a Minor Key
Sad Lisa
These Hallowed Halls

Old Los Angeles
Death of the Zanjero
Death of the City Marshal
Death of the Chinese Field Hands

Mrs. Sperling
A Nose for a Niedeman

Brenda Finnegan
Tyger, Tyger

Romantic Fiction
White House Rhapsody, Book One and Two

Fantasy and Science Fiction
A Ring for a Second Chance
But World Enough and Time

And I would be honored if you left a review for this and any of my books on GoodReads or any other retail site. It really helps.

About
Anne Louise Bannon

Anne Louise Bannon is an author and journalist who wrote her first novel at age 15. Her journalistic work has appeared in Ladies' Home Journal, the Los Angeles Times, Wines and Vines, and in newspapers across the country. She was a TV critic for over 10 years, founded the YourFamilyViewer blog, and created the OddBallGrape.com wine education blog with her husband, Michael Holland. She also writes the romantic fiction serial WhiteHouseRhapsody. com, Book One of which is out now. She is the co-author of Howdunit: Book of Poisons, with Serita Stevens, as well as author of the Freddie and Kathy mystery series, set in the 1920s, and the Operation Quickline series and Tyger, Tyger. She and her husband live in Southern California with an assortment of critters.